Rescued By the Spy

Rescued By the Spy

Laura A. Barnes

Laura A. Barnes

2018

First Printing: 2018

ISBN: 9781072863410

Laura A. Barnes

www.lauraabarnes.com

Cover Art by Cheeky Covers

Blurb by Emily Waskel

Editor: Polgarus Studios

To: William-I know you said we never have to say the words Thank You. But I am saying them anyway. Thank you for believing in me and pushing me to succeed. Also thank you for the countless hours I have been wrapped up in this book.

Prologue

Six months earlier

"**YOU WILL BE SAFE** here. I will come back later with help."

"He needs help now. This cave is not a safe place for us to hide. Shears will discover us here."

"I will handle Shears. You look after Charles, and this will soon be over."

"Over for whom. You? Me? This is far from over, and you know it. We need to get him medical treatment now. I have done everything I can for him."

"Only a few hours more. Do you think I care to see him suffer? It is for his safety and yours that I keep you hidden."

"If you do not return by midnight, I will seek help on my own."

"Agreed. Do you have the jewels in safekeeping?"

"They are concealed where no one will find them."

"Keep those and him protected. I will return for you both soon."

"See that you do, or I will make it known to everybody where your loyalties lie, then you will be the one who will have to stay hidden."

"Do not threaten me," he snarled.

"It is not a threat, but a promise."

With that he left the cave, Raina watched as he vanished along the beach, his dark black clothes blending into the night. The arrogance of that man exhausted her. He was too sure of himself and the games he played. But she knew he played the most dangerous of all games, a game that held too many lives in his hands. Raina only prayed that tonight the deception would end. She was tired of living on the edge.

Hearing the moan coming from the back of the cave, she hurried over to the sound. She gazed at the man who lay in agony and fever on the blanket that covered the ground. She swallowed the lump in her throat and blinked the tears away. It tore her up to see him in pain. She had tried to nurse him back to health, but his wounds were too severe. There was nothing she could do. He needed a doctor.

Lowering herself next to him, she brushed the hair away from his eyes and whispered soothing words. When he opened his eyes at the sound of her voice, she waited as he attempted to focus on her.

She stared as he drew the necklace from around his neck. It was a dark ruby nestled in diamonds. He pressed it into her hands.

"Wear this," his voice scratched out.

Raina tried giving it back. "No, I couldn't."

"Yes, you must. Go to the ball and find my sister, Ivy."

Raina dropped the necklace and backed away from him. What he wanted from her was impossible. He was not aware of her past with Thornhill. Even though she cared for him and wanted to help him, she could not risk getting caught.

He struggled to rise off the blanket. Raina knelt and helped him to a sitting position, resting him on the wall of the cave. Until Charles had his say, he would not rest.

"Go to the ball and find Ivy. If you wear that necklace she will realize you have information about me. She will help you. It is our only hope. You can trust her."

"But Maxwell will return."

"You and I both know Maxwell has his own agenda. I have no knowledge of what my friend has involved himself in, but he will only look out for himself at this point."

Raina was aware of what Maxwell was involved in, for she was involved in the same plot. She knew Charles spoke the truth though. Maxwell wouldn't be returning tonight or any other night. It was up to her to get the help Charles needed.

"I will go to the ball and return with Ivy."

He smiled at her as his eyes drifted shut. He whispered, "Thank you."

Raina watched as he went back to sleep. She lowered his body back to the floor of the cave, covering him with the blanket. She peeled the necklace from his fingers, slipping the ruby off the chain. As she dug into her bag, she found a black ribbon and slipped the ruby through the necklace. She tied the ribbon around her neck and made a choker of the jewel. It was not the only thing she drew out of the bag, as she also took out a long red ball gown. She did not fathom why she still carried the dress. Hope, she guessed. Hope for one day to wear it to a ball and dance with her prince charming. However, those days were never meant to be.

As she changed into the dress, she laughed to herself at the irony of the situation. She had found her prince charming, but he would not be at the ball with her. Nevertheless, she would attend the ball for him.

Leaning down she brushed a kiss across his lips. "Goodbye, my sweet Charles."

Gathering her bag, she left the cave in search of help. She wouldn't be returning to him. He was never destined to be hers. Still there was that small part of her that would disagree.

As he awoke at the touch of her lips on his, he heard her whisper goodbye. He watched the ravishing creature she'd turned herself into disappear from the cave. She was a dream in red silk. A dream that had kept him alive these last couple of months. A dream that he would make a reality as soon as he was well. He closed his eyes and drifted back to sleep. His last thought was of her—she and him sharing more than a mere kiss.

Chapter One

Six months later

IN THE BACK CORNER of the tavern, he sat there and studied as his fellow man made fools of themselves in their drunken debauchery. He never quite understood how, as ordinary people, they wanted to lower themselves to this behavior. As he waited patiently for news of any kind, he observed as the men drank themselves into imbeciles.

Lifting the mug to his mouth he took a long swallow of the disgusting ale. It tasted like soap water. Drinking it quickly, he swiped his lips on the sleeve of his coat. He wanted to spit the brew onto the floor, but he resisted as the barkeep scrutinized him with suspicion. He banged the mug on the table and nodded at him for a refill.

The barkeep kept an eye on Charles as he spoke to a man at the bar. They exchanged words as the stranger glanced over his shoulder, looking Charles over. After they spoke a few more words, the man made his way out the tavern door. The barkeep shouted for the serving girl to bring him his refill.

Charles propped back in his chair, rocking it on its back two legs. When the tavern girl approached him, he landed the stool on all fours. She leaned over, placing his ale before him, lowering her bosom in his face. When she rose, he was able to catch an eyeful of her breasts spilling out of her tight dress. Her corset pushed her breasts up tight and high while her dress laid low, right above her nipples. One quick tug and they would fall out into his hands if he so desired.

She tipped his hat back so she could look into his eyes and smile. "Is there anything else I can get for you, sir?"

Charles pulled her hand away from his face, tightening his grip. When she gasped in pain, he realized he needed to play his part better. To distract her, he drew her in his lap, nuzzling her neck. When she purred and went soft against him, he sensed she had forgotten the pain he inflected on her a few seconds ago. To continue his seduction, he traced his fingers across the neckline of her dress, his finger dipping inside to trace along her nipples.

"What is your name, darling?"

"Bessie."

"There is a lot you can do for me, Bessie, but maybe after your shift is done?" He raised his eyebrow in question.

"I get off in a few hours, I have a room above we can use." She told him as her hand wandered down to his lap.

"Well, Bessie, that does sound promising. In the meantime, do you think you can help me with some information?"

He continued to caress her as he saw her look back and forth between the barkeep and him. As a stranger in town, he was under suspicion. If questions were asked to too many people, it could draw unwanted attention upon himself. He nodded his head to the barkeep and smiled as if he enjoyed what was being offered in his tavern. That appeared to pacify the barkeep that he was a stranger passing through the village wanting a night's enjoyment before he left.

"Bessie?"

When she noticed she was not being watched anymore, she nodded.

"Now, Bessie, I do not want to get you in any trouble with your boss. So, when I ask you a question, just play along with me, okay, honey?"

Bessie looked back to the bar again and realized that Ray was no longer in sight. She couldn't afford to lose her job at the tavern, but she was so lonely for a man. It had been ages since a fine-looking bloke like this one had paid any attention to her. The sea captain who was in last week scared her, and she escaped his clutches by faking an illness, but next time she would not be so lucky. He was due back in port any day now, and Ray had promised her to the captain.

"Have you seen any other strangers in town besides myself?" he whispered in her ear.

She would not admit to him about the sea captain. Her life depended on it. The owner of the bar was involved in illegal activities with him, and she had overheard their plans. She shook her head while looking over her shoulder again.

Charles felt her grow tense in his embrace. Her body shook from the fear of something or someone, and he had a sense about who that was. He pulled her back into his arms and nuzzled at her neck, feeling her relax again.

"I can protect you, Bessie. You need say a single word. If the question I ask you is correct, stroke your hand along my arm. Do you agree?"

Bessie raised her head to stare into the stranger's eyes. He did not seem as dangerous as the other men coming into the tavern. More of a charmer than anything. She decided to trust him. He might be able to help her escape before it was too late. She lifted her hand and let it glide down his arm.

Smiling at her, he lowered his head again, pretending to kiss her. "Has there been any unusual activity in town within the last few weeks?"

Her hand caressed his bicep, shaping it to her palm.

"Have there been other strangers in the village?"

Moving down his arm, she wrapped her fingers around his wrist.

"Anyone by the name of Shears?"

Her fingers tightened on his wrist as her body grew tense in his arms again. She raised frightened eyes to his as she slid off his lap.

"I need to get back to work, sir," she explained as she let go of his arm.

His arm snaked out quick, grabbing her by her wrist.

"A few hours you say?"

She nodded as she picked up his empty glass. He dropped her wrist and swatted her on her backside playfully.

"Well, Miss Bessie, I will wait here for you; then we can use that room of yours for more fun later." He winked at her.

Bessie smiled at him, forgetting he frightened her with his questions. His smile held many promises she wanted to enjoy. She wandered back to the bar with the empty glass, smiling over her shoulder at him.

Charles raised his glass at her when she looked back at him. He continued to smile, looking her body up and down in appreciation. When he noticed her blush, he knew he had her convinced that he only wanted a good time. He would wait around here until he could go to her room, then he would get the answers he desired. She knew a lot more than she was letting on, but something—someone—had frightened her. He was close. If he was near, then so was she.

~~~~~

She watched him from the stairs. Her heart had not stopped racing since she'd seen him walk into the tavern. He was in danger, and she had no way to warn him. If she did, it would blow the cover she had worked so hard on, and she was not going to lose what ground she had gained just because her heart wanted to betray her. Why was he here? Didn't he know Shears wanted him dead? Why was he so bent on trailing him? Was he looking for her too? That was only wishful thinking on her part, the kind of thinking that could only get her into trouble. He would want nothing to do with her, not after he knew her part in kidnapping him, which he probably knew by then anyway. After all, she was captured by his brother-in-law.

Thornhill would have told him how she was behind the plot to kidnap him and how closely involved she was with Shears to bring the terror to England. It did not matter that she had nursed him back to health and tried to thwart Shears's terror plans.

He looked healthy as if he had made a complete recovery. The bruises had disappeared from his face. He was even more handsome than she could imagine.

As he leaned back in his chair, she watched as he smiled at Bessie. Her breath caught as she saw the charm that overflowed from his smile. When his smile reached his eyes, they lighted up in enjoyment. She never got to enjoy his smile, as he was always in too much pain. Even when his pain receded, they were always in too grave of danger to have a reason to smile.

Another emotion began to take place as she saw him flirt with Bessie. When he pulled Bessie onto his lap, nuzzling at her neck, she felt angry. Not just angry, but betrayed. How could he pull another woman into his embrace and share intimacy with her? Did the words and kisses they share not mean anything to him? Obviously not.

She watched as Bessie stroked his arm and listened as he told Bessie he would join her in her room later. *Well we will see about that, won't we, Mr. Charmer?* She planned to wait for him in Bessie's bedchamber.

Chapter Two

CHARLES SAT THERE NURSING another ale as he checked out the comings and goings of the tavern. A lot of men spoke with the barkeep, then headed to the rear of the tavern, where they disappeared for a few hours then left through the front again. Every man took notice of him. He recognized none of the blokes as ever working alongside Shears. But Thornhill had most of Shears's gang thrown in Newgate. The captain had to round up a new crew, but there were still a few of Shears's men left who would recognize him.

He tried to blend in with the other inhabitants of the bar by drinking and playing cards. As he pulled out his pocket watch, he realized that the hour drew toward ten o'clock. He had himself a date for information. Bessie seemed frightened, but he knew that she had the evidence he sought. Charles needed to draw that information out without sleeping with her. He knew that was what she sought, and it might be the only way she would give him what he searched for.

Looking toward the bar for any sign of Bessie to join her in her room, he only saw another tavern wench that looked to give birth at any moment. He grimaced to himself as he saw her lift a tray of drinks to distribute. She was small in nature, except for the burden she carried. Her hair was pulled back and wrapped up in rags. When she glanced up, he noticed her face covered in red blotches and that she had a mole that stood out on her cheek. She met his eyes and glared at him, then swiftly looked away.

Charles shook his head in confusion at that glare. What did he do to cause that? He sure hoped that Bessie had information he could use to find Shears, because he did not want to charm the likes of that wench, even though it looked like she had already been charmed. By lord knows who, he did not envy that guy. Poor bastard.

He watched as she worked the tavern floor, handing out the drinks. For somebody so frightfully ugly, she moved with much grace. As she made her way over to him, he observed her movements. He did not order a drink, so he did not understand why she came his way. She set a glass of whiskey in front of him.

"For you, sir."

"I did not order this. You must have delivered it to the wrong table."

"No, I'm not mistaken. It is a gift from Bessie. She said to tell you that she is running late. You are to meet her in her room at eleven o'clock. She will be waiting for you there. Her room is the third door on the left."

"Well, tell Bessie I said thank you and that I cannot wait to enjoy our evening together."

The tavern wench let out a "Humph," as she walked away.

Charles Mallory stared as she sauntered away, her hips swaying with her light walk. She seemed quite a package, if you took away her hideous face. He brought the glass up to his mouth to sip the whiskey as he continued to watch her work. There was something familiar about her. He was unable to place her, and he did not recognize her voice. It was rougher than most of the men that he played cards with that evening. Yet something about her did not make sense.

"Didn't realize that kind of wench drew your attention?"

Embarrassed to be caught looking at the wench, he drank the whiskey down quickly, turning in his chair at the newcomer.

"What have you found out?" Charles asked, changing the subject.

"He is due back in town later tonight. He has been moving his shipments through this tavern. Sammy is keeping an eye out back. They are on to you. I overheard that they are not sure who you are, but once the captain gets here, they mean to find out," Jake answered.

Charles did not want to bring Jake and Sammy into this mess, but his brother-in-law, Marcus Thornhill, insisted. He agreed for his sister Ivy's sake. She had already embroiled herself in this mess once, and he did not want her meddling anymore. So, to pacify them, he brought along Thorn's men to help him in his search for Shears. They didn't know about his search for the girl. She was another story. If they could find Shears, she wouldn't be too far behind.

Charles motioned for Jake to take a seat and started dealing out cards.

"Was Sammy able to find out where they moved the shipments?"

"Yes, they are moving them near a warehouse in the docks. But they are going to do things different this time around."

"How so?" Charles asked as he pretended to play cards with Jake. He did not want to draw any added attention to them. Also, he did not want them to connect Jake and Sammy to him.

"They are not keeping the guns in the warehouse. They'll distribute them among the villagers that are taking part in this madness."

"When is this going to take place?"

"Sammy overheard them say near dawn."

"Then we burn that warehouse down tonight. That will draw Shears out of hiding."

"That is too dangerous, Mallory. This village is surrounded by his men. There are only three of us; that plan is a suicide mission."

"There is no other way. We cannot let those weapons get into anybody's hands."

Charles looked up and noticed Bessie beckoning at him to join her. He nodded to her as he slid his chair back. Jake turned around and saw the buxom blond waving over at them. Charles slid his hand into his pocket and threw a few coins on the table.

"Good hand, but a man needs to learn when to quit. Besides, I've got a pretty lady to meet." Mallory began to walk away when Jake grabbed at his arm.

"We don't have time for this, Mallory," Jake argued.

"Yes, we do. She has information on Shears. Wait for me out back. If I do not return in one hour, come find me upstairs. The room is the third door on the left, or so I have been told," Mallory hissed as he jerked his arm out of Jake's grasp and strolled over to the waitress.

Bessie grabbed him and rushed them up the stairs to her bedroom. As they entered, they were met by the ugly waitress from earlier. She was sitting on the cot in the room, rubbing at her feet. She lowered her dress quickly when they hurried in, but not before Charles got a look at her slender ankles. They looked soft and curved perfectly with her feet. For being as far along as the waitress was, he expected her ankles to be more swollen. Ivy constantly complained of her swollen ankles due to her pregnancy in her letters to him. He figured it was a common ailment among pregnant women, but that didn't seem to be the case with this girl.

"Sally, go below and help out Ray. I need the room for a spell. I have entertaining to do this evening," Bessie told the girl as she ran her hand along Charles's arm.

"Not tonight, Bessie. My feet are aching. Ray doesn't want me working in the bar."

"He won't notice you tonight, he will be too busy. You promised you would fill in for me for a couple of hours."

Sally rose from the cot, slipping her feet into her slippers. As she held her back, she waddled over to the door, glaring at Charles all the way. He really was a cad. For him to fall victim to Bessie's charms so easily only proved that running from him was the best thing she did for herself. If this was how he wanted to spend his time, Shears would find him. It would be no fault but his own. Opening the door, she looked over her shoulder one last time to see Charles looking at her suspiciously as he pulled Bessie into his arms.

Charles watched as the waitress glared at him as she walked to the door. One would think that the ol' girl was jealous of Bessie here. Why? He did not understand, as he never showed her any attention. There was no reason to. Somebody already had from the looks of things. Poor soul, whoever that fool was. Raising his eyebrow at her in question as she paused at the door, he waited to see what she would do. Sensing that she only got angrier at the devotion he gave to Bessie, he decided to give her more. So, pulling Bessie into his arms, he began to lower his head to kiss her. When he heard the door slam shut, he looked up to see that she had left. Looking at Bessie, she had her eyes closed and was leaning into the kiss that he was going to deny her. He hated to disappoint her, but he could not bring himself to do the deed.

Lowering his head, he kissed her on the cheek. Pulling away, he loosened himself from her hold, wandering around the room. He noticed the threadbare curtains and bedsheets. He grimaced when he looked at the filthy bed, knowing that was how Bessie thought they would spend their time. However, Charles had other ideas. Turning back to Bessie, he saw her pouting, and he needed to lead her on until Jake came to his rescue.

Smiling, he walked over to the only clean thing he saw in the room and sat down. Lying on the cot, he inhaled Sally's scent. It was fresh compared to the stench of the rest of the room. Realizing that he focused too much on the ugly wench, Charles mentally shook himself to focus on his task this evening.

"Bessie, dear, fix me a drink."

Bessie went to her side cupboard and fixed him a drink. Charles watched as she poured something out of a jug into the dirty glass that she pulled out. Bessie slid onto Charles's lap with the drink. Bringing it to her lips, she slowly sipped the brew, gazing at him as she drained the glass. She lowered the glass as her tongue slid out and licked her lips. *Ah, the poor wench thinks she is being sexy, but she's saved me from drinking out of that disgusting glass*, Charles thought to himself.

"Bessie, you're being a tease aren't you, my dear?"

"You are the one being a tease. I thought you wanted my company tonight?"

"I do, Bessie, which is why I am here."

"Then why don't we go over to my bed, and I can show you what fun I can be."

"I don't want to rush, Bessie. I prefer to take things nice and slow. If you know what I mean."

Charles brought his fingers up to her neckline, sliding his fingers through the ribbon and unweaving them from their hoops. Spreading her dress open wider, he traced them along the opening. Her eyes grew heavy with desire.

"Tell me about the men who have been new to town. Do they work for a man named Shears?"

Charles felt Bessie tense in his arms and knew that he had to distract her more. He nuzzled her neck as he continued to touch her. Her body began to relax into his again; he questioned her more.

"Yes, they gather here. They use the tavern as a meet between the docks and their warehouse. I don't know what they are transferring, but I know that it is dangerous."

"Have you ever seen Shears?"

Bessie quivered in Charles's arms. Charles drew back and saw that she had gone as white as a ghost. She shook her head and pulled herself out of his arms.

"I do not want to talk about him."

"I can protect you from him; you must trust me, Bessie."

"Nobody can protect me from him."

"What do you know?"

She continued to shake her head. Charles tried to pull her back into his embrace, but she fought him. Bessie rose from the cot and paced the room, rubbing her arms.

"He is an evil man, Bessie. My men and I can protect you. Give me a chance."

"I think you need to leave. If anybody knows that you are in this room, they will kill me. I overheard Ray discussing you. They sent for Shears. He will be here soon."

"My men are waiting outside. Come with me, and we will protect you."

"No, you must—" Bessie was interrupted by pounding on the door.

"Bessie, you get your lazy ass downstairs now. You know how I hate that fat cow serving drinks to the men," Ray yelled through the door.

"I will be down in a minute, Ray."

"You get down there now, and hurry; Shears will be here any minute, and I told him you will be available for him tonight. And none of those shenanigans that you pulled last time. He is a powerful man that I do not want as an enemy. Do I make myself clear?"

Charles watched as Bessie whitened even more than she had earlier as she answered, "Yes."

He stared as she slowly pulled herself together, lacing her dress back into place. She moved to the mirror and fixed her hair.

"Wait until I have gone below and sneak out down the back stairs. I will keep Shears busy. You must leave this town tonight."

"Bessie, please let me help you."

Bessie left the room, ignoring his pleas.

Charles sat on the only chair in the room. The rickety chair shook under his weight. As he leaned on the two back legs, his eyes searched the room. He was in no hurry to leave. His anger toward Shears only made him delay running. Besides, he was always two paces ahead of Shears finding him. As he had been tracking Shears these last few months, he'd learned his routines, and they never differed; that is why staying ahead of him was so easy. Tonight would not differ from any of the other nights.

His eyes landed on the pregnant girl's cot. He noted the differences between her cot and Bessie's. Something was not right. Her small area looked too neat and organized for a tavern wench. Her cot was made, and her clothes were neatly stacked beneath. A small treasure box was partially hidden under her garments, like it was put away in a hurry but not completely. Charles remembered that they had surprised the wench when Bessie and he had entered the room. Had she been looking in the box before they came into the room? If so, what was worth keeping it hidden?

He landed the chair on all fours as he came to his feet. Walking over to her cot, he knelt to pull the box from underneath her garments. As he looked at the clothes, he spotted what good condition they were in. Bringing them to his nose, he smelled her fragrance. Now why would a tavern wench have such sweet-smelling clothes? From his experience, women in this position never concerned themselves with cleanliness or kept their dresses in such pristine condition. Things did not add up with this woman. Who was she?

Pulling out the box, he observed what delicate condition it was in. The keepsake box was small and engraved with crowns and wands. In the middle of the box sat an emerald. The cut of the emerald was exquisite. Charles laughed. What was he thinking? It wasn't real, just a believable paste job. Still, he ran his thumb across the jewel. For a paste, it appeared smooth to the touch. Opening the treasure, he saw an inscription card sewn into the cloth that protected the inside of the box.

To our Fairy Tale Princess,

May all your wishes and dreams come true.

Love, Mama & Papa

Charles smiled to himself, imagining the young girl opening this gift from her parents. She must have been loved unconditionally. What was the wench doing with something so precious? Only children of wealthy parents were given such a gift as this. The trinkets were too costly for the poor. Each piece was always handmade, and hours of work went into the delicate detail of these boxes. Was she a thief? Who did she lift this from? He looked inside the box at the various treasures, hoping to find a clue who this belonged to. As his fingers dug through the items, he came up empty. They were only objects from a young lady who believed in fairy tales—a dry pressed rose, a broken bracelet, a couple of buttons that looked too big to belong to a young girl—maybe her father's—and a blue handkerchief. He lifted the fabric out of the box for a closer look. As he unfolded the material, he heard a commotion outside the door.

Charles swiftly stuffed the handkerchief back into the box and closed the lid. He slid the case inside the front pocket of his coat. He moved her clothes back into place and straightened up the mess, not wanting her to be aware that he spied on her.

As he rose to his feet, the door flung open, and the pregnant wench rushed into the room as she headed to her bed. The same cot that Charles kneeled in front of. He came to his feet and tried to distance himself from where he was, but he was caught. Upon seeing him, she stopped abruptly. She looked between him and her cot, and her eyes went to the place he was moments ago. When she saw that nothing had been disturbed, she relaxed.

"Waiting for Bessie are ye?"

Charles watched as she moved over to the cupboard and pulled out a glass. She poured a drink from a different jug than Bessie had used. He thought that she was relaxed, but her hand shook as she poured the liquid into the glass. Wondering why he made her so nervous, Charles moved closer to her. She had him curious. As she saw him come near her, the wench tried to move away, but he cornered her up against the cupboard.

She felt trapped in more ways than having him trap her against the cabinet. Her eyes darted around the room, looking for something to distract him with so that she could make her escape. When she came into her room and had seen him near her cot, her heart wanted to leap out of her throat, but when she saw nothing out of place, she became calm. Since he had not confronted her with what was hidden underneath her clothing, she realized her secrets were safe. If he found what she had hidden, he would recognize who she was.

"We didn't get to finish what we started. Since she isn't returning, maybe you care to take her place?" Charles baited her.

She knew that he was trying to make her more nervous than she already was. Her hands shook as she raised the glass to her lips. She decided a small sip would calm her nerves before she responded to him. But before she took a sip, he wrapped his hand around hers, pulling the glass out of her hands.

"What do you think you are doing?" she asked as she rubbed her hand. She felt a spark as his hand touched hers.

Tilting his head back, Charles took a drink. The whiskey burned as he swallowed the fiery liquid. He soon felt the warm glow settle in his gut. It was nothing compared to the warm glow that he experienced when his hand had brushed hers. It was as if a flow of heat had passed between them, which did not make any sense, as she was not his type at all. Not only was she hideously ugly, but she was also an angry woman, and he always tried to avoid that type.

"Whiskey is not good for you to drink."

"Why isn't it? And who are you to tell me what I can't drink?"

Charles nodded his head toward her stomach. "That is the reason you don't need the drink."

Sally stared at her stomach in confusion. Wrapping her hands around her middle, she raised questioning eyes up to him.

"It is not good for the babe."

She turned away from him to get her thoughts under control. How could she forget about the babe? His presence in this small room turned her thoughts and actions into mush. She was forgetting her mission. She needed to pull herself together and focus on what had to be done. Turning around, she expected him to be right behind her, but he had wandered over to her cot. She watched warily as he lowered himself to lie on it. He sprawled back on his elbows, regarding her. His eyelids dropped lower.

"So, what do you say, my dear? From the looks of things, this is something you enjoy," he said as he patted the space next to him.

Sally blushed at his assumption. He could not be farther from the truth, but who was she to correct him? She decided to play along with his little game. It would only last for a few moments more.

She smiled at him, showing him her yellow teeth and grabbing a hold of her stomach as she walked over to the cot. Sally laughed to herself as she took glee at the revulsion on his face from her smile and the bulk of her stomach. This was too much fun after all. Since he wanted to play this cat-and-mouse game, she was all too happy to play along. Leaning over him, she gave him a view of the swell of her breasts as she positioned her hands on both sides of his shoulders.

"Why not? I've had worse. But you might want to hurry. The last I heard, Shears and his men are planning to kill you tonight," she said as she ran her fingers through his lush blond hair, brushing it back from his face.

Charles grabbed her hand, tightening his grip around her wrist. "What do you know of Shears?"

Sally gulped at the pressure on her wrist. "I know that he wants to kill you."

Charles closed his eyes then slowly opened them. Something wasn't right. Was she sent in here to distract him while they plotted their plan to kill him? If so, it was working. What he couldn't understand was his attraction to this woman. Her breasts were hanging near his face, ready to fall out of her dress at the right tug if he so wanted them to. She smelled sweet, like honey. *I wonder if she tastes as sweet too.* He suddenly felt exhausted. Closing his eyes again, he shook his head to clear his thoughts. He needed to focus on Shears and what his connection was to this woman.

"Who are you?"

"Does it matter who I am?" the wench asked as she tried to tug her hand away.

Charles only tightened his hold more, bringing her off balance and causing her to fall on top of him. He brought his other arm around and held her trapped to his body. She fought to get out of his embrace but only caused herself to be crushed tighter to him. Raising his head, he captured her mouth in a kiss.

She was stunned as his lips caressed hers. It was powerful and shocking to her system. As she opened her mouth to protest, it was all the encouragement he needed. His tongue swept in controlling her with long deep strokes. Tasting her, licking her, devouring her. His tongue traced the outline of her lips, then slowly slid back inside, stroking her tongue with his. As he pulled his lips away from hers, he placed a gentle kiss on her lips.

Charles was also stunned at the kiss. If he wasn't lying down, it would have knocked him to his knees. He could taste and feel her reaction of the kiss. She did not take part in the kiss, but he sensed the response from her. Her body went soft against him, and he heard her moans. She did taste like honey.

Things had gone too far. She panicked and tried pulling out of his arms. Her knees came up and dug into his lap. Charles moaned and let her go. As she crawled off him, she fell to the floor. She quickly got to her feet and backed away. She held her hand up to her lips, following him with her eyes.

Charles groaned in agony from where her knees landed. He sat up slowly, doubling over from the light-headedness. Laying back down, he closed his eyes. Opening them again he turned his head and watched as she backed herself up to the door. He knew she was going to try to escape. He could not let her leave. None of his questions were answered by either woman tonight. Holding out his hand, he tried to focus on her, but she was becoming blurry.

"Wait, don't go. I need to talk to you," he slurred his words.

The wench shook her head at him in denial.

"I'm sorry, Charles," she whispered.

She saw Charles pass out on her cot. She had to get out of there before he came to. Rushing over to the bed, she pulled out her knapsack and stuffed her belongings into the bag. She watched as he slept. He looked so tired and worn out. Why didn't he stay in Margate and recuperate? He was on a fool's errand, chasing after Shears. He was only going to get himself killed. She could tell that he was still in pain from his injuries. She wished she could stay and take care of him again, but it was too dangerous for both of them. Why did he have to kiss her? The kiss almost blew her cover. Even though she didn't kiss him back, her body betrayed her.

Brushing the hair off his forehead, she let her fingers trail down his cheek. The bristles from his beard rubbed roughly against her fingertips. She traced his lips with her fingers before she lowered her head and lightly brushed her lips across his.

Standing up, she glanced around the room, checking to make sure that she left nothing behind. It was time to move on. Her cover would be blown, and her work was done in this town after tonight. As she paused in the doorway, she wanted to turn around for one more look. She fought herself not to turn. If she did, it would only make her long for something that was impossible for her to have. She yanked the door shut behind her as she walked away from him. As she ran down the backstairs, she heard footsteps racing up the other stairway. She paused as she listened to the voice of her nightmares. Pulling herself back into the shadows, she picked up her pace and swiftly made her way out of the tavern. She managed to escape both men in her life tonight. It was too close this time.

Chapter Three

"RAINA," CHARLES WHISPERED AS he awakened.

He sluggishly opened his eyes to the glaring sun. Moaning, he shut them and pulled the blanket over his head. He had the mother of all headaches. Charles didn't recall drinking as he tried to remember what he did the evening before.

Everything came back to him in a rush of memories. The kiss. It was her. How could he have been so blind to her disguise? He felt the connection to her but did not understand how or why. She was a fool putting herself so near to Shears.

As he rose out of bed, he bumped into the nightstand. His balance was off kilter. He knocked the tray to the ground with a clatter, the glass breaking. The door flung open at the racket. When Jake and Sammy saw it was only him, they shook their heads as they came inside, closing the door behind them. Neither one of them said a word. Sammy cleaned up the mess, and Jake sat in the only chair in the room, making himself comfortable. He stretched out his long legs, putting his hands behind his head and staring at Charles, waiting for him to speak first. When Charles refused to talk, Jake shook his head in disgust.

"Where is she?" Charles finally inquired.

"She who?" Jake asked back.

"Raina."

"How are we supposed to know her whereabouts? You are the one looking for her."

"I was with her last night."

Jake laughed. "No, you were with the waitress Bessie, and when she left, the ugly one entered."

"Raina was the ugly wench."

"I thought you had better taste than that, Mallory. This spy business has changed your style in women."

"You fool, she was in disguise. Where did she go?" Charles yelled to get his point across.

Jake sat up in his chair at the anger in Mallory's voice. How was he supposed to know the chit was in disguise?

"She left the room before we rescued you. She was headed to the back stairs. When we heard Shears and his men coming up the front, we realized we had to get you out of the room. When we knocked on the door, you did not answer. We found you passed out on the cot."

"She had a drink. There must have been a sleeping potion in it. I remember grabbing the glass before she drank it. I didn't want her harming the babe." Charles went white after his last comment.

It sunk in what he was saying. The babe. Raina was with child. The knowledge made him weak in the knees. He lowered himself to the bed as the realization of the danger she put herself through. It also made him question whose child it was. Was the babe his? He only remembered brief snatches of his illness, most of that time was still a blur. Did they sleep together during that time? Closing his eyes, he tried to recall, but he could only remember the flavor of honey on her lips from their kiss last night. He tasted her resistance, but he did not imagine her becoming soft in his arms. She was in danger.

"Where did she go?"

"She snuck down the back stairs. After that, we don't know. We grabbed you and left. By the time we came down the stairs, she disappeared."

Charles rose from the bed and started to get dressed. He had to locate her. She was his to protect whether or not she realized it. Even if the babe wasn't his, he would offer them his protection.

"Where do you think you are off to?" Jake asked.

"I am going to find her. She could not have gone far."

"You are not leaving, Mallory. We have strict orders to hold you here until nightfall."

Jake and Sammy moved to stand in front of the door to block his exit. Did they imagine they could stop him from searching for her?

"Instructions from whom? I don't answer to anybody but myself."

"Thornhill said to keep you here. He plans to meet us tonight at the pier. There is no way you can wander this village after last night. We will have to wait for word that he is here, then it will be safe to leave."

"What happened last night? Where are we? Also, why is Thornhill involved now?"

"Here is a safe house that Thorn used during the war—one that we desperately needed after last night. You're a dead man if any of the villagers see you."

"Why?"

"You don't remember a single thing from the night before?"

"I recall trying to talk Bessie into giving me information on Shears, then she went downstairs. When the pregnant wench came in, it was a battle of wills. Then the next thing I know, I'm waking up in this room."

"Bessie was murdered, Mallory, and they are pointing the finger at you, my friend."

"I never laid a hand on her. She left the room."

"Well her body was found in her room this morning covered in blood. Her throat, slit. Everyone in the tavern saw her go upstairs with you."

"But you saw she wasn't in the room when you rescued me."

"Yes, but who are we to be trusted? Two strangers in town who are not connected to you. They planted her body there after we left."

"Damn."

"You have made Shears an extremely powerful enemy, Mallory. He will stop at nothing to destroy you."

"You had better tell him the other good news," Sammy said with sarcasm.

Charles rubbed the back of his neck with his hand. Could it get any worse? In his line of work, the answer was always yes. It could, and it would. But if he could stop Shears, anything that happened would be worth it. The man had destroyed too many lives and continues to destroy more.

"What else happened?"

"The warehouse with the weapons burned to the ground."

"Well, that is good news. It was what I instructed you to do."

"It wasn't us, sir," said Sammy.

Charles looked between the men for answers. If they did not burn the warehouse down, then who did? Both shrugged their shoulders with no clue on who might have done the destruction. He closed his eyes as the truth hit him. It was her. She was bent on revenge.

"Raina."

"There is no way the girl did that, sir," Sammy tried to explain to Charles. "It was too elaborate of a fire for a mere girl to set."

"She is no mere girl, Sammy. She is the daughter of a general who fought under Napoleon. She is a woman set on avenging the death of her family. She is a danger to us all unless we can stop her," Charles explained.

They all contemplated the destruction she could do if they didn't find her and put a stop to her plans. The greatest threat was to herself. When somebody believed they had nothing to lose, they would put themselves into grave danger to achieve any goal.

"Where do we go from here, sir?" Jake asked Charles.

"We stay with the course of action. We trail Shears. Because wherever Shears goes, Raina will follow him. This time, you two will gather information while I look for the girl."

"How are you going to stop her? Thornhill tried the night we rescued you. He assumed he got through to her," said Sammy.

"I need the chance to speak with her. To try to reach out and help her understand she has to step back and let us do our jobs," Mallory explained.

"Jake, grab the necessary supplies, and Sammy, ready the horses. We leave here in the middle of darkness. Send word to Thorn that I will meet him in London in a week's time."

They nodded their heads at his direction and left the room. Charles walked to the window and pulled back the shade just enough for him to be aware of his surroundings. He observed the villagers as they continued with their daily routine, unaware of the danger that their country was in. It was his profession to protect these people, and he was doing a horrible job of it. He also needed to shield Raina from herself, perhaps most of all.

Nothing seemed to be out of the ordinary. As he looked up and down the street, he did not notice anybody watching his room. The women gossiped on the corner while the men worked.

He pulled back from the window, unaware he was being watched, that somebody was watching and waiting for him to make his next move. He had made himself vulnerable in too many ways. His head was not in the game. It was wrapped around a piece of baggage that could be his destruction. That made him a threat to himself.

~~~~~

They took off in the dead of night, riding their horses into the darkness. Keeping off the main road so not to be noticed, they made their way toward London. Mallory was aware Shears would have to go to the city to meet with his benefactors. Charles had thwarted him these last few months and knew Shears was short on funds. He also knew that Shears was headed to London and that Raina would follow him. He would find her there, and when he did, he would have to convince her to lie low. She must understand that there was a price on her head.

Mallory shifted on his horse and felt a sharp jab against his side. He reached into the inside of his coat and pulled out the jewelry box he found from the tavern wench. He opened the lid, looking at the contents with a whole new eye. The case and the items it contained began to make sense to him now that he realized Raina was the owner.

He smiled to himself as he imagined the little girl storing her most prized possessions in her keepsake. His smile turned to one of sadness as he sensed her pain at the loss of her parents and why she must treasure this so much. She was going to be very angry and upset when she realized that it was missing. Mallory had a few questions for her about the keepsake box and the items it contained when he found her.

Jake and Sammy pulled up on both sides of him, and he quickly slid the treasure back inside his coat.

"We are being followed. Only one rider from what I can tell," Jake said.

"Yes, I am aware. We have been trailed since we left town. He is keeping his distance from us. Let us continue on our way and pretend that we are none the wiser."

"I don't think we should take those kinds of chances, sir," Sammy argued.

"If the person's main goal is to harm us, he would have done so by now. He is acting alone; we will wait him out."

"Is it a he or a she?" Jake asked.

"It isn't her. She has already caught up with Shears. That is why we must hurry."

Mallory pulled ahead and raced his horse faster to their destination. Jake and Sammy followed suit. They didn't agree with his decision, but they understood he would not stop.

They rode for hours. Once dawn was beginning to break, Charles slowed down and walked his horse over to the river. Sliding off the horse, he let the animal take a much-needed drink.

"We will take a short break here. I will take the first watch. You two get some rest," Mallory told them.

Charles winced as he observed Sammy climb down from his horse and limp over to take a drink from the river. He felt awful for pushing the old man the last few hours. He realized that riding for a long period of time put Sammy in a lot of pain. The story of how Sammy acquired his injury was due to saving Thorn's life. As soon as they got to London, he would have to leave Sammy behind. He did not want to risk the old man's life going after Shears. He would not have that on his conscience too.

As he waited for the two men to fall asleep, he kept an ear out for their follower. He heard the rider pull off when they did. Where was he hiding now? Mallory snuck off in the trees, trying to draw out their visitor.

He listened to the snap of twigs off to his right. Circling back, he managed to get behind him. He viewed the man as he leaned up against the tree, his hand above his head. His other hand rested on his hip, drawing his coat behind his back. He had a hat on, pulled low over his face.

Pulling a weapon out of his boot, Mallory advanced on his enemy.

"Put the knife away, Mallory. I mean you no harm."

Mallory paused at the familiar voice. He'd assumed he was dead. There had been no sign of him as Charles trailed Shears, and rumor had it that Shears had killed him. But that was all they were. Rumors.

"Maxwell."

He waited for Maxwell to turn around and face him. But he was unprepared for what he saw. This wasn't the man who had been his partner the last few years. It was a man who looked like he was haunted by unknown demons.

"I heard you were dead. By the looks of you, I'm thinking it might be true."

Maxwell raised his eyes at his comment but didn't respond to it.

"Does everybody else assume that I'm dead?" Maxwell asked.

"You mean by everybody, the Crown?"

Maxwell nodded.

"They're skeptical. They only have the rumors from Shears to confirm it—not that he's the most trusted of men."

"Does Shears presume I am dead?"

"Well since he is the one boasting he killed you for double-crossing him, I believe so," Mallory commented. "Why are you following me, Maxwell?"

Maxwell shrugged his shoulders, his jacket scraping against the tree. Mallory hated when he did this. You constantly had to pull information out of him. He was always twisting things around to confuse people, to draw the attention away from him. This time Mallory was prepared and would wait him out.

"Well since you are here, you might as well keep watch. I'm going to catch some shut-eye before we ride again," Mallory said as he made his way back to camp.

Maxwell didn't respond but followed him back to the other men. When they returned, Jake woke up to take the next shift. Jake glanced between the two and advanced toward Maxwell. Mallory shook his head at him to back off. Jake stopped and glared at Maxwell and began to keep guard.

Maxwell slid down against a tree and leaned his head back. Sliding his hat to cover his eyes, he decided it was finally safe to get some sleep. He knew Mallory would have his back. Their friendship was a long withstanding one that stretched back to childhood. Charles might be mad and disappointed in him, but he would not turn him in. Yet.

Chapter Four

RAINA WAS AWARE THAT this was dangerous, but it was the only disguise that kept her protected while she gathered the information she looked for. Not only was it risky, it was her most insane idea yet. But if she pulled this off, she could get the evidence she needed and be in a safe environment. She was lucky to be alive, especially after her latest escapade. Her revenge for Shears was as strong as ever, but after what happened to Bessie, she knew she was fortunate to still be alive. While she had no love for Bessie, she felt sad another innocent life had ended at the hands of Shears.

She slowed her steps to a crawl. It would not do to get caught running along the hallway like a young maid. This time she must be careful and not make mistakes with her disguise. Charles must have seen through her cover at the tavern. Why else did he kiss her? Why, indeed? Obviously, she did not know him as well as she thought she did, considering the way he snuggled up to Bessie and then was kissing her the next minute. He was a cad. She only got to view the sick Charles, the one who depended on her for survival, not the rake he most certainly was.

Raina walked into the nursery and watched the young lad play with his ships. He was acting out the part of the captain as he took over the pirate ship. How ironic that the boy wanted to recreate the very thing he had escaped from. He hero-worshiped his new father and was pretending to be him. The child was lucky to have found a new family that cared for him as the Thornhills did. He was the one bright spot to this dilemma with Shears. An innocent who had managed to survive his clutches. Hopefully, it continued this way for the young man.

"Well, Tommy, it is time to wash up for dinner. You will have to leave your privateering for another day," Raina said.

"Ah, but I was just getting to the good part. I was going to take over Shears's ship and plunder his crew," Tommy complained.

Raina fought back a grin at that scene. "Well you can plunder away tomorrow. Your parents are on their way up before they attend a dinner this evening."

Tommy jumped up with a smile and rushed over to the washstand. He chattered on about his battle to her as he washed his hands. Raina walked around the room, picking up toys and putting them back on the shelves as she listened to his story. It was a shame he wasn't older. They could sure use him in their fight.

When Tommy finished washing up, Raina brushed his hair and straightened his clothes before the Thornhills arrival. She was finishing tucking in his shirt when they walked into the room.

Tommy ran across the nursery, right into Thornhill's embrace. Marcus Thornhill swept him up into the air and tossed him, catching him in his arms. They both laughed at the excitement. Ivy Thornhill watched with loving eyes at their display of antics. Tommy explained his story about the battle. Thorn set Tommy on the floor, following him over to his battleground, and lay on the rug to play with the young lad. Ivy wandered over to the sofa and lowered herself gently on the cushions, leaning back and resting her hand on the small swell of her stomach. The lady was a few months pregnant with their first child. She settled into the couch with a serene smile on her face as she regarded their play.

Raina stood off into the shadow of the room, observing their family in envy. She didn't begrudge them, but she wished for a sense of family for herself. But alas, she had none. She was alone in this world with only herself to look after. At one time, she only felt hatred for Thornhill. She had thought he took her last remaining family from her, so she wanted to destroy him and everybody he loved.

She learned that he was not the enemy she believed him to be. She was directing her anger at the wrong man. The same man she was helping at the time. The man who had taken her whole family from her. The man she had set on destroying. Now instead of destroying Thornhill, she would use him to destroy the one who had ruined her life and who was still trying to harm this family.

When Raina looked toward the couch, she found Lady Thornhill watching her. She smiled at Raina as she rubbed her stomach with one hand and patted the sofa with the other.

"Please join me, Mrs. Whitlow. I think these two will be at this battle for a spell," Ivy said.

Raina made her way over to the sofa at a slow pace. She made sure that her steps resembled an older lady with extra weight. She had taken the padding from her last disguise and distributed it throughout her costume. Instead of looking pregnant, she looked like an elderly woman with a few added pounds.

Thornhill jumped up from where he was playing and offered her his help to the couch.

"My apologies, Mrs. Whitlow, I was caught up in the excitement from young Tommy here. Please let me help you," Thorn explained while reaching for her arm.

Raina flinched at his touch. Thornhill looked at her in puzzlement, but Raina relaxed her arm under his. While she recognized he wasn't her enemy anymore, old habits were hard to let go of. At one point she hated this man with a vengeance and was still somewhat angry at the treatment she suffered from him earlier this year. It would take time to forgive him. The last thing she needed was to draw any suspicion her way.

"I apologize, my lord. My old aches and pains are bothering me. The damp weather does that to this ancient body," Raina tried to explain herself out of her predicament.

"No, I am sorry, Abigail. We have you doing too much for us."

Raina lowered herself next to Lady Thornhill.

"Nonsense, I am most grateful for the position you have given me, Lord and Lady Thornhill."

"Please, we have asked you to call us Thorn and Ivy," Ivy said.

"That is most improper and not a good example to show Tommy."

"You are correct, Mrs. Whitlow. How about when we are alone we shall be on a first name basis? When other servants or guests are around, we can refer to each other with our proper names. Will you agree to that?" Ivy replied.

Raina nodded her head in acceptance. She liked this woman. Ivy was kind and caring to those she loved. She had welcomed Mrs. Whitlow into her family with open arms. While Raina felt guilty for her deception, she knew this was the only way. This was her only connection to Charles. Under any other circumstances, Raina believed they could have been true friends.

"Well I have a brilliant plan then. I will take Tommy with me tomorrow to finish getting the ship ready to return to Margate, and Abigail can join you tomorrow, Ivy," Thorn explained.

He lowered himself on the arm of the sofa, pulling Ivy's hand from her stomach up to his lips. Thorn kissed Ivy's palm as he smiled at her in amusement.

Ivy let out a chuckle and grinned back at him.

"You wouldn't be trying to maneuver your way out of joining me tomorrow, would you, my dear?" Ivy asked.

"Of course not, madam. I am only looking for a way to give Abigail a rest from our son."

Ivy laughed at his excuse and leaned back into him as he curved his arm around her. They smiled into each other's eyes, lost among themselves.

"Please say yes, Mama. I want to help Papa with the ship," Tommy said.

"What do you say, Abigail? Care to accompany me tomorrow for a relaxing day of shopping and visiting friends?" Ivy laughed.

It was hard not to relax and enjoy herself with this young family. They caught her up in their enjoyment of life.

"I would love to join you tomorrow, Lady Thor—" Raina started to finish but stopped at the clearing of throats from Thorn and Ivy.

"Lady Ivy, I mean."

"Ivy will do, Abigail."

"Ivy, I would love to help you with your day tomorrow."

"Well then it is agreed. We are off to the ship tomorrow, young man. But for now, you need to give your mama kisses. We are off to the Blackstone's for dinner," Thorn told Tommy.

"Night Mama," Tommy said to Ivy as Ivy wrapped the boy into her arms.

Ivy gave him a kiss on the cheek. "You go to bed for Abigail tonight when she tells you, and we shall see you in the morning."

Thorn and Ivy said their goodnights and left for the evening.

"I will get our dinner trays brought up, Tommy. Why don't you read a chapter of your book and I will be right back."

"All right, Abigail. Then after dinner will you continue your story?" Tommy asked.

"Yes, as I put you to bed, I shall tell you more," Raina promised.

Raina saw Tommy settle into a chair by the fire with his book as she left the nursery. She slipped quietly down the stairs and pressed herself up against the wall outside the receiving room. She knew the Thornhills were taking a carriage to the Blackstone's with Ivy's father, George Mallory, the Duke of Kempbell.

"So, what have you heard? Is Charles out of danger?" George asked Thorn.

"Yes, Jake and Sammy were able to get him to the safe house. I got word this afternoon that he refused to wait for my help and is riding to London. I expect him by late tonight," Thorn explained.

"He is wanted for murder. London is the last place he needs to be seen," Ivy complained.

Raina gasped at this information. Murder? Who was he to have murdered? She knows in her heart that Charles could never kill anybody.

"Those charges won't stick with the Crown; the War Office realizes he was framed. Shears has set him up good this time," Thorn explained.

"Why was he in the tavern girl's room?" Ivy asked.

"Jake said she knew information about Shears, but when she left the room, Charles was duped by another serving girl. She drugged him and disappeared. Jake got Charles out before Shears came."

"That doesn't explain how the girl was murdered," said George.

"I guess Shears saw the girl's death as a perfect opportunity to frame Charles. He was the last one seen with the wench," Thorn said.

"Well hopefully by tomorrow morning Charles will be here and can tell us his plans," Ivy replied.

Raina walked away toward the kitchen to have their dinner sent to the nursery. This was horrible. She knew Bessie was dead but felt in her soul that Charles did not murder her. *When I left him, his friends were on the way into the room.* This had Shears written all over it. Poor Bessie, she only ever wanted to be loved. While she was not the cleanest person to share quarters with, she had a kind heart. When Ray didn't want her working up front, Bessie always stuck up for her. It saddened her that Shears snuffed out another life for his evil agenda.

But Charles was coming to London. *He must have the same information on Shears that I do. I will have to make myself invisible when he is near.* Raina's heartbeat quickened at the thought of seeing him again. Would he be able to see through this disguise too? No, it was too believable. He did not know it was her at the tavern, at least she didn't think he did. She hope he made it home to his family safely, but she had to focus on her mission. To destroy Shears. She could not let her feelings jeopardize everything she had accomplished in the last few months. Especially for a man that fancied any lady. Not just ladies but tavern wenches too. The man was not worth it, no matter how he made her heart feel. Raina tried to convince herself of these feelings for Charles Mallory with no success. She still longed to gaze upon him and to savor his lips upon hers.

She continued to the kitchen for Tommy's dinner. On her way back, Raina was lost in her thoughts of Charles, and wasn't paying attention to the direction her feet were taking her. She jostled into a solid form. As she looked up, she stared at the Duke of Kempbell as he reached out to steady her. His hands grabbed hold of her shoulders to stop her from falling. They were gentle on her, but they still made her tense at his touch.

Backing away from him, she dropped into a curtsey.

"Please forgive me, Your Grace," Raina said in a soft feminine whisper.

"No problem. It is the fault of an old man not looking where he was going," he replied.

Raina realized that she had not disguised her voice when she asked for his forgiveness.

"Oh, posh, sir. You are younger than I." Raina deepened her voice with a crackle to it.

"You must be dear Mrs. Whitlow that is helping my Ivy out with young Tommy."

She nodded her head in acknowledgment. Raina relaxed when she realized that he did not notice her voice change.

"I hear nothing but positive reviews on your performance. I know that daughter of mine; she will not rest for a minute. I am forever appreciative on any help you can give her in her time of need."

"Oh, I am the one who is grateful for the Thornhills giving an old lady a chance at employment. They are a joy to work for, and Tommy is a delight. Speaking of Tommy, I must see to his supper and bedtime. If you will please excuse me, Your Grace." Raina dropped into another curtsey as she tried to remove herself from his presence.

"Let me see you to Tommy before I leave. I want to give the boy good news." George Mallory offered his arm to Raina to go with her to the nursery.

She slipped her hand through his arm and walked with him. Trying to keep herself relaxed, she was thankful for the silence as they made their way up the stairs.

When they entered the room, he patted her hand and gave it a gentle squeeze. When she raised her eyes to his, he winked at her. Startled, her eyes opened wider in surprise. Before she could reply, he was being charged at by Tommy.

"Grandpa George, do you want to see my battle?" Tommy asked.

"I've heard rumors of this battle. I must leave for dinner with your parents. Would you like me to join you in this battle tomorrow when your Uncle Charles gets here?"

"Uncle Charles is coming to town?" Tommy asked.

"Yes, my boy, he will be here tomorrow. You can regale us with your battle when he arrives."

Tommy jumped up and down in excitement.

Raina watched the two, admiring how the older gentleman had accepted the orphan as his grandson. There were no false airs. He took joy in the young lad. There was more to this family than Raina had given them credit for. She thought they were all alike, all the pompous aristocrats. But she was becoming to see they were a kind and generous family. It made her want to know them better. However, she would never be given the chance to know them in the intimate way she desired.

The duke gave Tommy a hug goodnight and bowed to her.

"Until tomorrow, madam," he said as he walked out of the nursery.

Raina settled Tommy at the table as the servants laid out their dinner. They enjoyed a quiet meal. Tommy told her exciting stories about his Uncle Charles, the hero. She sat there savoring everything she could discover on Charles Mallory.

After dinner she got him ready for bed and settled into a rocking chair next to his bed.

"So where did we leave off, young man?" Raina asked.

"The part where the maiden trapped the evil captain in the cave," Tommy answered.

"Oh yes. Well, the evil captain swore revenge on the young maiden, but she knew she had won for the day. She needed to get back to her patient so she…" Raina continued with the story as she watched Tommy drift off to sleep.

Chapter Five

ON THE OUTSKIRTS OF LONDON, the party of four stopped to rest their horses. As they came near a creek, the men slid off their mounts. Jake and Sammy walked the horses to the water as Mallory and Maxwell stretched their legs. Maxwell nodded for Mallory to follow him. Jake watched as Maxwell led Mallory around the bend of the creek and off into the trees. He made to trail them, but Mallory waved him away. Jake shook his head at this, in obvious disagreement.

Mallory understood Maxwell was not out to harm him, so he followed. When they had gotten deeper into the woods, Mallory called out for Maxwell to stop.

"What is it, Zane?"

"You need to call off this witch-hunt. You are going to get yourself killed."

"No, I will kill Shears, and it would be in your best interest not to keep yourself aligned with him. Because after he is dead, you run a huge risk of getting yourself killed too," Charles told him.

"You don't understand. He has deep backers protect him. You can never get close enough. For every warehouse you burn to ashes, he is putting up two more. You cannot handle the power these men hold. I can't keep protecting you."

"I have stopped several of these men. It won't take me much longer to put the rest of them away."

"There is one man more powerful than the rest who support him. You won't be able to reach him."

"Who is he?"

"If I knew, I would stop him myself," Zane growled as he kicked a tree in his frustration.

"I can't end this fight. I have to see this through to the finish. He will regret what he did to me and to those that I love." Charles swore his vengeance.

"I can keep him away from you and your family if you quit this pursuit of Shears," Zane promised.

"Those I love will never be safe as long as he walks free. Plus, I must keep the pressure on him to keep her protected."

"She is in a secure location."

"How do you know? Where is she?" Charles asked.

"She couldn't get any safer than where she has hidden herself," Zane answered.

Charles advanced on Zane. He was desperate for any news on Raina. He grabbed him by his shirt and pulled him forward so they were face to face.

"Tell me where to find her," Charles demanded.

"I promised not to betray her whereabouts, she—" Zane began to explain.

They did not hear the approaching footsteps until it was too late. Charles and Zane were grabbed from behind as three men attacked them.

They yanked Charles by his arms, pinning them behind his back. While the man behind Zane seized him by the neck and proceeded to choke him. The third man came around Zane and laughed while Charles struggled in his friend's arms. He smiled at Charles, revealing two gold teeth in front.

He pulled back his arm and sucker-punched Charles in the stomach with one fist. Then his other arm hooked to the side to land a blow into his ribs on his left side.

With the wind knocked out of him, Charles sank to his knees, gasping for air.

The gold-toothed man circled the men, rubbing his fist into his other palm.

"The boss ain't going to be too thrilled to discover you consorting with the enemy, Maxwell," Gold Tooth said as he struck him across the face.

Zane's head flew backward from the force of the punch. He managed to hit his captor in the face with the back of his head. Caught off guard, the captor staggered a few steps before dropping his hold on Zane. Zane took advantage of this, sliding his knife from his boot as he continued after him. The two fought on the ground, his enemy wrestling to stay away from the weapon. They rolled next to a tree, where Zane pinned his attacker. Pulling his knife back, he slid it into the captor's side. He watched as the man struggled to breathe.

Zane struggled to his feet as he turned to help Charles when he saw Gold Tooth and his friend taking turns with Charles, thrashing him. He didn't stand a chance. Gold Tooth himself was over six feet, five inches and pure muscle. The other was no small bean himself. Together they were a force to be reckoned with.

With his arms clenching his stomach, he made his way over to Mallory to help. Gold Tooth saw him approaching out of the corner of his eye when his hand swung backward and caught Maxwell on the side of the head. After regaining his balance, he went after them again, going after the partner instead. He lowered his head and ran into his side.

The partner stumbled backward, letting go of Mallory. That was when Maxwell took the lead and thrashed the cohort, showing no mercy. But Gold Tooth was not done with Mallory yet. He continued his assault.

Zane saw Jake and Sammy come into the clearing. They doubled up on Gold Tooth, knocking him over to the ground. When Zane had finished on the partner, he moved to help them. They had Gold Tooth's arms pulled back and were tying him to the tree.

"Get him out of here. I'll finish with this one," Maxwell ordered them.

"No, we will take care of him and you," Jake countered.

"Don't be daft, man. Leave before the others show up to finish us all off."

"Jake, we don't have time to argue. We need to get him help. He's worse than before," Sammy shouted.

"This isn't over, Maxwell, Thornhill will come for you. You have trapped Mallory for the final time."

"I didn't set him up. We were ambushed," Maxwell tried to explain.

"Humph," Jake replied.

He knew Thornhill's men did not believe him. But he felt Mallory recognized the truth.

"Go."

Jake and Sammy lifted Mallory and carried him to the horses. Maxwell listened to his moans as they walked away. He turned around to tie up loose ends.

"He will kill you for this." Gold Tooth spat out blood from his mouth.

"No, he won't Goldy. He will have your hide for attacking us. I was in the middle of receiving valuable information for him. He will not take too kindly when he hears about this," Maxwell smirked.

"Information my arse. I overheard you calling Mallory off the fight against Shears."

"That is your word against mine, friend. You grasp nothing of being a double agent, do you? You must keep their trust, and to keep their trust you must sympathize with them. That is what I was doing before you so rudely interrupted us. Tut tut."

"You lying bastard. You can't lie yourself out of knowing where the girl is. I heard that part. You know her whereabouts. The captain will sure love that piece of information. He can't wait to get his hands on that one."

Maxwell did not take his bait. He finished tying him and his friends to the tree. As he stood up, he wiped the dirt onto his pants.

"Yeah, the captain is excited for her. The blond one he had last year was too much of a prude for his taste, but this one he thinks will be feistier," Gold Tooth baited him.

Maxwell clenched his teeth in anger, trying for control. He knew Gold Tooth referred to Ivy. The thought of any lady in Shears's grasp made him furious. Maxwell would make sure that Shears never got hold of Raina or Ivy. If Raina was captured, they would murder her. She was the one behind the destruction of Shears's plans. He would make her suffer before he killed her. Maxwell was not going to let that happen to Raina, even if it meant offering himself as a sacrifice.

"Tell him he knows where to find me," Maxwell told him before he punched him out.

Chapter Six

RAINA AWOKE TO A commotion outside her bedroom door. She heard the servants hustling up and down the hallway. Voices rose as instructions were belted out. As she slipped from bed, she covered herself in her robe, pulling the wig over her hair. When she opened her door a crack, she peeked out to see Thorn and his men carrying a body toward a room at the end of the hall. Ivy was following them, still dressed in her evening gown. Raina saw Ivy crying.

"Will Charles be all right, Thorn? How badly is he beaten?" Ivy asked between sobs.

"I don't know, my love. I have sent for the doctor. We will find out soon," Thorn answered as he carried the body into the bedroom.

They shut the door after they entered the room. Raina listened to Ivy's sobs as Thorn tried to comfort her.

"Right this way, doctor. He took quite a beating. He hasn't awoken since." Raina saw Thorn's man Sammy leading the doctor to the bedroom.

Raina continued to listen as they entered the bedroom. Thorn led Ivy from the room for the examination. She watched as Ivy paced along the hallway in a nervous fret.

"Stay calm, dear. This stress isn't good for the baby." Thorn halted Ivy, pulling her into his arms.

They stood there quietly holding each other. She knew their thoughts were on the man who was bloody and beaten in the room beyond.

He bent his head, drawing her lips in a sweet, gentle kiss. It was a kiss filled with compassion.

Raina closed her door and leaned back against it. She tried to slow her heart from racing. He was injured again. Was it her fault? She realized when she set the fire it would draw the attention to him, but she trusted him to disappear. She had observed his patterns these last few months, and he always left town after she destroyed Shears's warehouses. What happened this time?

For her own peace of mind, she needed to see him. Raina undressed and slipped into Abigail Whitlow's disguise. She adjusted the extra padding before she slid into the oversized dress and thick shoes. Pulling the wig off, she twisted her long black hair into a bun and then put the wig back on, securing it to her head with pins. She lit a lamp by the mirror and applied makeup to her face. When she stood up, she looked herself over to make sure she wasn't forgetting something in her disguise. Assured she looked the part, she moved to the door, grabbing her shawl along the way.

Wrapping the shawl around her shoulders, she stooped as she opened the door. With a slow pace, she walked into the hallway. By the time she emerged, the hallway was empty. The bedroom door was open, and the Thornhills and the Duke of Kempbell were whispering among themselves. Raina tapped on the door quietly.

"Can I be of service?" Mrs. Whitlow asked.

"Please come in, Abigail. I am afraid Ivy's brother, Charles, has gotten himself into a bit of trouble. Can you sit with Ivy for a spell? George and I need to investigate a few things, and I don't want to leave her alone," Thorn asked.

"I will send for tea while we look after young Charles here," Abigail replied. Her eyes examined Charles, looking for any signs of movement from him.

Thorn bent his head and whispered into Ivy's ear. He leaned over to place a kiss upon her head before he walked away.

"Thank you, dear Abigail. We are forever in your debt. If you can, please try to get her to lie in bed. This cannot be good for the babe," said Thorn.

Mrs. Whitlow nodded in agreement.

Thorn and the duke left, and Abigail yanked the bell for the servants. When the butler arrived, she requested tea to be delivered to the room. She then pulled up to a chair next to Ivy and waited with her. They both watched as he lay there sleeping, wincing at every moan that left his lips, feeling his suffering as their own.

"He does all this for her," Ivy whispered.

"For her?" Mrs. Whitlow asked.

"A woman he does not even know, but from what he feels here," Ivy said as she placed her hand over her heart.

"A woman he loves, how romantic. May I ask who the young lady is?" Mrs. Whitlow questioned.

"Her name is Raina LeClair. It is a true mess, Abigail. I'm not so sure she is worth it, not when he keeps ending up injured."

Raina tensed when she listened to her own name. Her face paled as she glanced at Charles, then back at Ivy, not believing what she heard. Charles loved her? Impossible.

"Does he love her deeply?"

"I don't know, Abigail. I do not even think he knows. It is a long story. I don't even know where to begin," Ivy explained.

"Well why don't you tell me while we wait for your brother to awaken."

"Yes, maybe it will help to talk to somebody different," Ivy agreed.

Ivy told Abigail how Charles went searching for the woman who had kept him captive earlier this year. She explained the whole mess with Charles and Shears. Meanwhile, a maid returned with tea and sandwiches. As Abigail served them, she listened to Ivy tell her story of falling in love with Thorn again, all while they tried to uncover the terror plot that Shears was bringing upon England.

"Raina had your brother held captive?" Mrs. Whitlow asked.

"She worked with Shears in the beginning. But I believe she began to have feelings for my brother and her allegiance switched. We think she was also working with Zane Maxwell to help bring Charles to safety."

"Why do you believe Charles loves her?"

"He told me he has feelings for her and that he needed to find her to explore these feelings. Charles has never felt this type of connection."

"It could be nothing but infatuation, my dear."

"I do not believe so anymore. He won't stop in his search for her, and in doing so, he will get himself killed by Shears."

"Maybe she does not have feelings for your brother the way he feels for her. Maybe it would be best if your family could convince him of this."

Ivy laughed bitterly. "Oh, believe me, Thorn has tried."

"How so?" Abigail bit out.

"Thorn tried warning Charles off Raina. That she was a woman bent on revenge, but Charles argued that she was a woman who was hurt and needed his love to heal."

Raina was shocked at the story Ivy told her and didn't know how to respond. Could what Ivy said be true? Did Charles truly have feelings for her? If so, it would not matter. The only way to avenge her family was to destroy the man responsible for it. If casualties happened along the way, then so be it. Loving him was impossible, anyhow. She may never heal from this destruction. Nor did she want to. The anger and hurt kept her going. Without it, she could not carry out what she had planned. Maybe her heart would heal when this was over. But for now, she was not ready.

She knew Thornhill was angry with her for holding Charles captive. He might be furious with her after this incident with Charles, even though she had nothing to do with his current injuries. Raina no longer held Thornhill responsible for the death of her father, but he still was not her friend. It upset her to learn he was against Charles looking for her. While she did not want Charles chasing through the countryside in pursuit of her, it comforted her to know somebody cared for her. She decided that she could use Thornhill's dislike toward her to her advantage.

"Maybe your husband is right, my dear. Charles's best interest should be to move on from this girl."

"I think you might be right, Abigail. How will we convince him to forget her?" Ivy questioned.

"Talk to your husband and come up with a plan to stop Charles from chasing Raina LeClair. I am sure the two of you together can persuade your brother that he needs to let her go."

Raina saw the effect her words had on Ivy. If Ivy could convince Thorn to keep Charles from looking for her, Raina could complete her mission without the life of Charles Mallory on her conscience. She watched Ivy lay her head back against the chair and close her eyes. She brought her hand up to her mouth and yawned.

"Why don't you go to bed? I will sit with your brother," Mrs. Whitlow offered.

"Oh, I can't let you do that, Abigail."

"You must rest for the baby. I will stay with him until your father returns."

Ivy yawned again. "All right. You are a cherished friend, Abigail."

Raina smiled a bittersweet smile at Ivy. She bore such guilt for deceiving her, but this was for the best. She would be gone in a week. That was all the time she needed to finish her plans. Then Charles would be healed, and she could disappear to a different place and reappear as a different person.

Raina helped Ivy to her feet and assisted her. She called for Ivy's maid to help her to her bedroom. As Ivy walked away, she slid back into the room, closing the door quietly. Walking over to the side table, she turned the flame lower on the lamp. Flames from the fireplace lit the chamber. Their light danced in between the logs of wood, bathing the area in a soft glow.

Pulling the chair closer, Raina sank into the cushion, relaxing for the first time in ages. She gazed at him as he slept. She placed her hand on the bed, sliding her fingers in between his. The warmth of his hands blanketed her cool hands. Her whole body seemed chilled to the bone. Not from the cold, but from fear. Fear of being discovered, fear of her plans, but most of all, the fear of being alone. But she wasn't alone right now. She had him.

She laid her head on his shoulder and closed her eyes. Breathing him in, her body relaxed more. She felt the brush of his breath as he blew on her hair. Bending her neck back, she looked upon his face. His eyes were closed, but she imagined them open. She remembered them being dark green, unless he was teasing her, then gold flecks flickered through them. She wished she could see him smile now.

Raina raised her hand and brushed the lock of hair from his eyes. She then traced his face with her fingers, gently brushing across his sores.

She wanted to take away his pain with her touch. He moaned from her caress. It wasn't a moan of pain, but one of relief, as if her touch was healing him. She slid her fingers across his lips. He opened them slowly and sighed.

Before she realized what she was doing, she raised her head off his shoulder and brushed her lips across his, softly kissing away his pain. Her tongue traced the outline of his lips, tasting the blood from them. She moaned at the agony he was suffering. She felt his lips move against hers, and she pulled back, staring at his mouth. She looked up and saw that his eyes remained closed.

Whimpering in pain, she heard him moan a name. A name that made her freeze above him.

"Raina."

He could not be asking for her. She did not quite believe Ivy's story of Charles's affection for her. It was not possible he had any love for her. They barely knew each other.

Raina pulled away. She had to leave before he awakened. It would not look good if she was caught lying with him. There was no believable explanation she could give for that.

Before she rose from the bed, Charles's arm wrapped around her waist, drawing her body across his. Raina put her palms on his chest and tried to pull herself from him, but his arms were iron bands holding her to him.

When she looked up, her eyes locked with his. They were bloodshot and unfocused. She had to get away from him. But before she could move, he raised his head and kissed her as tenderly as she kissed him. As if he was trying to heal her wounds. The wounds that were not visible. The wounds she kept open to protect herself from hurting any more than she already did.

His lips brushed across hers, coaxing them wider. When her lips opened underneath his, he slid his tongue in to brush across hers. Long slow strokes to comfort her, to draw her pain into him.

Raina moaned as her body relaxed against his, sinking into his kiss and arms. She kissed him back softly, afraid to want more. But when the kiss became more passionately. It scared her, and she tried to pull away. Her elbow dug into his side, and he let out a scream.

She scrambled off him and off the bed. Staggering back, her knees hit the chair. Her body sunk into the cushion, so as not to be discovered.

She stared as he brought his hands to where her elbow had slammed, his eyes clenched in pain. He let out long moans and curses. As he tried to pull himself up, Raina watched as dizziness overcame him. Charles reached out his hand to her for help.

She shrank deeper into the chair. She wanted to comfort him, but she froze in fear that he would recognize her. If he did, she was ruined.

"Who are—" he started to say when he collapsed back onto the bed.

Raina was still too afraid to move. She watched him as he lay there, his chest rising and falling in deep shallow breaths. When he made no sudden moves and his eyes stayed shut, Raina gradually moved closer to him.

His face was pale from his exertion. When he still did not move, Raina realized that he had passed out. She reached out and gently brushed the hair back from his forehead, her hands trailing through his thick, golden hair. Her fingers shook as she caressed him.

She sank to her knees and slid her hand into his, her fingers clasping his. She laid her head on their enclosed hands. A tear slid along her cheek, sliding between their fingers. More tears followed as she wept for the aches he endured.

Pain caused by her. If what Ivy said was true, then she was the reason he was hurt. Could she give up her revenge on Shears to keep Charles safe? What meant more to her, destroying Shears or keeping Charles safe? She knew what her answer was without having to decide. She realized what she had to do.

She had one more mission to complete while she was in London, then she would disappear forever. Raina could never be with Charles; he was too good for her. There were things from her past as well as her present he would never understand. Things she did out of survival. He deserved a better woman than her.

Looking up, she watched him as he slipped into a deeper slumber. She only ever saw him injured and sleeping. A few months ago, as she nursed him back to health she watched him while he rested. There was something about him that put her at peace.

He always brought her a sense of calm. When he awoke, those green eyes searched into her soul. Raina was always lost to the magic of Charles Mallory. Lost to something she was too afraid to explore. All she had to do was reach out and grab the magic, but everybody knew magic was not real.

Charles tightened his fingers, the slight pressure startling Raina out of her musings. As she looked up, she saw he still slept but was muttering in his sleep. When his fingers squeezed tighter, Raina gasped. He began to thrash on the bed. Not wanting him to break open his injuries, she tried to calm him.

With her free hand, she ran slow soft strokes over his chest and whispered to him that he was well. She continued this, and he calmed, hoping that he could return to his restful slumber.

"There, there Charles. Please settle," Raina soothed.

He quieted at her voice and touch, relaxing back into a peaceful rest. She watched as he went back to sleep. Pulling her hands away, she lifted the blanket to cover his chest but was taken by surprise at his whisper.

"Raina."

Backing away from the bed, she watched him, hoping that he was not awake. When his eyes didn't open, she knew it was time to depart. She was on the verge of losing her cover.

Hurrying to the door, she opened it to leave. When she took one last look over her shoulder at Charles, she walked right into the duke.

"Steady, Mrs. Whitlow." He reached out to stop her from plowing into him.

Raina pulled back. She always seemed to be running into him. With her eyes downcast, she murmured, "I am sorry to run into you again, Your Grace. I am going to retire for the evening. Let me get a maid to sit with your son."

"No need, madam. I will sit with him for a spell. You need your rest. You will have a full day tomorrow with Ivy and my grandson."

Raina curtsied. "I bid you goodnight then, Your Grace."

"Let me walk you to your bedroom," he offered.

"Oh, no. I will be perfectly fine." Raina tried to escape his company.

"Nonsense, I wouldn't be a gentleman if I didn't escort you safely to your room."

Raina conceded and let him draw her arm through his as they made their way along the hallway. Still lost in her thoughts of her time with Charles, she did not realize that they had stopped at her bedroom door. When she glanced up, it was to see the duke regarding her with patience and a kind smile.

He reached out and patted her hand.

"All will be well, my dear," he said as he opened the door and gently guided her into the room.

Raina watched as he closed the door. As she looked at her hands, she realized that they were bare. She had forgotten her gloves.

In her hurry to find out what had happened with Charles, she had not completed her disguise. Gripping her fingers together, she tightened her hold at her incompetency. Releasing them, she slid one hand over the other, her fingers gliding over her hands as she wrung them in fear. Her heart was racing with the knowledge that Charles's father had figured out who she was. She knew that he knew. His comment revealed that he saw right through her.

Panicking, Raina paced back and forth across the carpet. She needed to get out of there. She had never felt so trapped. Part of her wanted to remain near Charles. The other part realized her cover was blown and that she had to flee before she was caught. But she had nowhere to go. This was her final act of revenge to stop Shears. If she left London, she would never have the chance again.

She sat on her bed, defeated. If she left, she would not be able to follow Charles's recovery. Closing her eyes, she pictured him lying on his bed in pain. His body beaten and bruised. She could still hear his deep shallow breaths as he tried to bring fresh air into his lungs. Raina knew he would recover. He always did. This time she could not nurse him back to health. That hurt the most. Even though it was not her place to give him care, it did not stop her from longing to be his caregiver.

However, she could as Mrs. Whitlow. His father did not call her out. He saw through her deception but did not draw others to her attention. If he had wanted her gone, she would have been thrown out by the footman standing guard in the hallway. Instead, he had walked her to her door and patted her hand in condolence when it was she who should have been consoling him.

Raina rose from the bed and began her pacing again, but this time it was to think. A plan was beginning to form in her mind. It was brilliant, and it might actually work. Now all she had to do was hope that the duke would not expose her before she could complete her task.

Chapter Seven

CHARLES AWOKE, FEELING A sense of déjà vu. He winced as he pulled himself up, resting his back against the headboard of the bed. He leaned his head back and closed his eyes as his hand massaged his side. He rubbed his sore muscles and reflected on how he ended up this way again. Charles shook his head. He realized he only had himself to blame.

He was the one who kept putting himself in these predicaments. That and trusting the wrong people. He lowered his guard twice within the last couple of weeks, which made him lucky to be alive. He might hurt like hell, but at least he was still breathing.

He swung his legs over the edge of the bed. As he stood, a wave of dizziness caught him unaware. He fought the weakness and came to his feet and walked a few inches over to the chair, sinking into the cushion.

Charles leaned his head back, closed his eyes, and took a deep breath. His sides ached. Shears's men sure knew how to pack a punch. Damn Maxwell. If he wasn't so caught up in arguing with him, he could have been more aware of his surroundings. But Maxwell distracted him with the one thought that kept him from keeping his mind on their location. *Did he count on that? Is that why he was distracting me? Was it a setup? I cannot believe it to be true.* But was it? Was Maxwell in so deep with Shears, he could no longer be trustworthy? No, it was an act. Wasn't it? He tried to help me escape from their clutches. If it wasn't for Maxwell, he would be dead in the woods. He had to continue to believe Maxwell would act right in the end. He was the only one who did.

Which left him with his other problem. Raina was consuming his every thought. Not only when he was awake, but in his dreams too. Last night had seemed so real. He could taste the sweet honey on her lips as they kissed. The touch of her in his arms as she melted into their kiss. He even dreamed that she caressed his injuries, as if her touch could heal them.

Which was impossible. She wasn't anywhere near here. She couldn't be crazy enough to step a foot in this household. She had to realize Thorn did not trust her after what she pulled. But Ivy would let her in. She knew what Raina meant to him. Was she real and not a dream?

Impossible. He had to get a grip on reality. Raina LeClair was a mystery to him, one he was beginning to believe he would never solve. He let himself feel the excitement of the unknown when in reality, she was of questionable character. Things did not look well for her.

First, she kidnapped him and held him captive. Second, she worked for Shears. Even now she was destroying him. And third and foremost, she was a spy, always in disguise and messing with his emotions. Emotions that were clouding his judgment. Emotions he needed to get in check before his family got hurt. They had been through enough already. It was time for him to finish his mission. Then and only then could he pursue his feelings for her. But for now, he needed to focus on ending Shears and his backers.

Shifting in the chair to ease the pain in his side, his hand became tangled in a soft piece of fabric. He pulled it out from underneath him. A woman's shawl. It must be one of Ivy's old shawls. The material was faded in color. At one time it was a vibrant blue, now only pale in comparison. The wrap was mended many times. Why his sister was keeping such an old and worn out shawl was beyond him. It must hold sentimental value to her. He had to make sure that a maid returned it to her room. If it held special meaning to her, he had no wish for it to be discarded.

As he raised the shawl to put on the side table, he caught the scent from it. It was not his sister's usual perfume; it was much heavier, but sweet at the same time. He brought the shawl up to his nose and breathed in the fragrance. The scent reminded him of something. He had smelled it before, but he could not place it. He shut his eyes and sniffed the perfume again. Charles tried to picture where and when he had detected the aroma.

That was when he was caught. Ivy decided at that moment to walk into his room, unannounced as usual for her.

"What are you doing, brother dear?" Ivy asked.

"Nothing," Charles said pulling the wrap back onto his lap.

"That is not what I saw. It looks as if you're smelling something."

"Just catching a whiff of your old shawl. It is not your usual scent, dear sister."

"The shawl does not belong to me. You are sniffing dear Mrs. Whitlow's shawl. The horror if she was to walk into your bedroom. Can you imagine her embarrassment?" Ivy teased him.

"Well I am sure your dear Mrs. Whitlow has enough manners to knock first, unlike someone else I know."

"I see you are recovering nicely. And to think of the tears I shed for you last evening."

Charles felt guilty for putting Ivy through more worry. Especially in her condition. He was acting like an ass to her.

"I am sorry for being such a bore. Please forgive me," he begged.

"It is fine, Charles. I realize you have much on your mind. I am glad you are well. You had us worried last night."

"As you can see, I am no worse for wear. How are you?"

Ivy laughed as her palm caressed her stomach. "How do I look? I am as huge as an elephant."

"My adorable elephant," Thorn said from behind her, putting his hand over hers and pulling her back up against him.

Charles watched the affections of his best friend and sister. For two individuals who had kept their feelings from each other for so long, it was comforting to watch their love for one another. He wanted that in his own life.

Thorn settled Ivy into the chair next to Charles. He walked over to the windows and opened the shades and cracked a window. The crisp morning air sent a chill through the room.

"We are being watched, my friend," Thorn told Charles.

"By whom?"

"I was hoping you could tell me. I have never seen these blokes."

"Shears has himself a whole new crew since you threw the rest of his outcasts in Newgate."

"These men are not with Shears. They are too polished and professional," Thorn explained.

Charles rose from the chair and made his way to the windows. He opened the window wider and leaned out, pretending to take a deep breath of fresh air. He noticed the two chaps watching the house, blending into the scene on the street. To any other observer, they were two gentlemen taking a stroll along Mayfair. But in truth, they were hired killers.

He understood that coming to London would be dangerous. There was a price on his head. Those connected to Shears wanted him dead. Charles knew too much. He should never have come back here. He put Ivy in direct contact with danger, but he had to come. Charles sensed Raina was here and who the next person on her list was, for it was the next name on his list too. He had to convince Ivy to leave London.

"You need to take Ivy back to Margate," Charles told Thorn.

Thorn nodded. "I have made arrangements."

"How soon?"

"Tomorrow at the latest."

"Please come with us, Charles," Ivy begged.

"I cannot leave, but I will follow soon."

"Will you promise me you will be safe?"

"As safe as I can be," Charles promised.

Ivy struggled out of the chair when Charles helped her to her feet. As he pulled her up, he wrapped his arms around her and gave her a hug.

"Did you find her?" Ivy whispered.

Charles shook his head no to her unanswered questions. Ivy squeezed him in her understanding of his heartache.

"Well I will finish packing and work on getting Tommy to pack his toys." Ivy turned to leave the room but turned back to pick up Abigail's shawl.

"I will return this to Mrs. Whitlow before she finds you sniffing her belongings again."

"Who is this elusive Mrs. Whitlow And why was her shawl in my room?" Charles asked.

"She is the wonderful companion we employed to help me with Tommy's care. Abigail sat with you last night after I retired," Ivy explained as she left the bedroom.

"Sniffing the hired help's clothes?" Thorn inquired with a smirk.

Charles rolled his eyes. He was not going to enlighten his friend, best friend or not. How could he even explain it? It made him appear delusional, and they would question if he got hit harder on the head than they thought.

"Do you want me to take care of your shadows?"

"Don't bother. Only more will emerge. Just get Ivy out of town, and then I can handle them. They won't harm anybody until I show my face. I'm sure he has thugs at every one of my old haunts."

"Jake says Maxwell is behind this latest incident."

Charles shook his head in denial.

"Still protecting him, are you? He will get you killed."

"Maxwell saved my life. He was not involved with the attack."

"He is not to be trusted."

"It's complicated, Thorn, but you know in the end that he can be trusted."

"Why do you keep standing up for him? Especially after everything he has put you through."

"Because, in the end, he is my friend. Through all the smoke and mirrors, at the end of this war he will still be my friend. He is your friend too. We have been through too much not to see this through to the end. He may appear as the enemy, but you know what he is and who he is—our friend."

"I hope you're right."

Chapter Eight

THE HOUSE WAS BUSY packing up the belongings to take to Margate. It was in an uproar because of the speed at which they had to leave town. Every maid and footman was busy packing and loading up the carriages.

Charles listened while Ivy gave directions left and right. If anyone could pack in a hurry, it was her. He observed as everybody scurried to do her bidding. They did not hurry out of fear, but because they respected her. Ivy always treated the hired help with kind words and interest. She knew every one of them on a first name basis and all about their families. How she was able to keep everything straight was beyond him.

Charles wandered down the hall toward Tommy's room. He wanted to spend a few moments with his new nephew and figured this would be a good time while he was healing and hiding from Shears.

As he came upon the room, he saw an older woman reading to Tommy. She must be Mrs. Whitlow. She was precisely as he pictured, an old woman. She was padded in the middle, obviously from eating too many biscuits with her tea. Her dark gray hair pulled back tight in a bun, and wrinkles outlined her face. She was a typical lady's companion and governess.

Charles leaned against the doorjamb, listening to the story as she read. Her soft voice melodic to his ears. He was drawn in to the voices of her characters. She would change the tone of her voice for each, and they would come alive she told their story. So, wrapped up in listening to her, he was surprised when Ivy spoke from behind him.

"First you are sniffing her clothing, and now you are looking all moon-eyed over her. Are you sure you are feeling better? Maybe I should call the doctor and have him check your head for more injuries. You do know that she is old enough to be our grandmother," Ivy whispered in a stage voice to him.

Charles glared over his shoulder at his sister, but she brushed past him and into the room. As she walked over to Tommy, she ruffled his hair and spoke softly to Mrs. Whitlow.

Mrs. Whitlow looked up at Ivy's words and closed the book. Charles noticed her hands were shaking as she tried to lay the book on the table, but the book slipped and fell to the floor. She bent Bending over and picked up the hardcover, laying it back on the table. She smoothed her hand against her skirts and nodded to Ivy.

Ivy handed a letter to her, and Mrs. Whitlow slid it inside the front pocket of her dress.

"Charles, let me introduce you to our Mrs. Whitlow. She has been such a help to us," Ivy said.

"Mrs. Whitlow, my brother Charles Mallory."

Mrs. Whitlow dropped into a curtsey. "It is a pleasure meeting you, My Lord. I heard much about you from the Thornhills and Tommy."

When she rose from her curtsey, Charles grabbed her hand and placed a kiss upon her glove.

"The pleasure is all mine, madam. I want to express my extreme gratitude for sitting by my side last night. I was not myself, and for that I apologize."

Her hand shook inside his grasp. His mention of last night caught her unaware. She raised her eyes up to his, panicking that he knew who she was. Her body relaxed when she noticed he was a gentleman being gracious to somebody he was meeting for the first time. Lost in his smile, she was caught off guard when he was trying to pull his hand away. She had somehow tightened her grip on his hand. Dropping her hand, she backed away and gathered her things.

"I will take care of that errand for you, Lady Thornhill."

"Thank you, Abigail. We will see you at dinner." Ivy dismissed her.

Abigail dropped into a curtsey then exited the room. Charles watched her go, puzzled by their exchange. Something about her did not seem right. *When she returns, I might try to have a few private words with her.* Anybody new in their life was under suspicion as far as he was concerned. It could do no harm to find out whose side she was aiding.

"How long has Mrs. Whitlow worked for you?" Charles asked Ivy.

"For almost a week now. She has been a godsend. Why do you ask?"

"Just curious, my dear," Charles remarked casually. He did not want Ivy to be aware of his suspicions.

"Curious about what?"

"Nothing. So, Tommy, I hear you have quite a battlefield set up in here. Why don't you show me how you plan to battle?" Charles asked Tommy, trying to distract him from Ivy's prying.

"It is right over here, Uncle Charles." Tommy led Charles over to the battlefield and explained the pieces to him.

Charles smiled indulgently at the young lad, caught up in his excitement. He remembered playing like him when he was a child. His battlefields also took up half the nursery.

Tommy told him a story that Mrs. Whitlow was telling him. Charles listened at the tall tale, enthralled with the danger of the story. That Mrs.

Whitlow seemed to be quite the story teller. He guessed an imagination would come in handy for a woman in her position.

"The spy is following her, so she tricks him with her disguise. Giving him a sleeping potion, he falls asleep as she makes her escape. Then the heroine rides off on her horse after she sets the evil pirate's warehouse on fire. Mrs. Whitlow promises to tell me more of the story tonight." Tommy finished with his tale.

Charles started putting the pieces together as he listened to Tommy's story. It could not be, but it was. It was staring him in the face the entire time.

The dream from last night was real. The shawl, it had her smell. Her voice as she read Tommy a story was the voice that got him through his kidnapping last year. Her hand, as he held it in his moments ago, had shook. It was her. Damn, she fooled him again.

"Where did she go, Ivy?" Charles demanded.

"Mrs. Whitlow?"

"Yes, Mrs. Whitlow, since that is what she is calling herself now."

"Well what else would she call herself? What is the matter, Charles?"

"She would call herself Raina LeClair if she was herself and not running around in disguises all the time."

"Mrs. Whitlow is Raina? That is impossible."

"It is possible, and I need to find her right away. She is in danger. Now where did you send her?"

"I sent her to drop off a letter to the Blackstones. I was apologizing for leaving their dinner party early last evening because of you."

"How could you send her there of all places? She is walking into a trap!" Charles shouted.

Thorn and his father came running into the nursery. Thorn rushed to Ivy's side and pulled her protectively into his arms.

"What is this shouting about?" Thorn questioned Charles.

"She sent Raina to Blackstones."

"Raina? Charles, Raina is not here," Thorn tried explaining to him

"She was in disguise and had you, of all people, fooled."

"Who? How?"

"Raina is Mrs.—" Charles began.

"Whitlow," his father finished

Their eyes turned to George in confusion and betrayal. He sighed and made his way over to the rocking chair and sat down. Looking at Ivy, he nodded his head over at Tommy, who was watching them with curiosity.

"Tommy, I heard cook made your favorite cookies today. Why don't you run along to the kitchen and have her give you your snack?" Ivy suggested.

"Sugar cookies my favorite. I hope she frosted them too." Tommy ran from the room toward the kitchens.

"How long have you known?" Charles asked his father.

"Last night I walked her back to her room after she sat with you for a spell. I patted her hand, and she was not wearing any gloves. Her hands were of a lady in her youth, not those of an aged governess she was portraying. Her eyes held a look of deep sadness and fear. I figured it was her in disguise."

"Why did you not inform us of this?" Thorn questioned.

"I was trying to protect her and keep her safe. I thought if she knew we guessed who she was, she would flee. But if we pretended that she was fooling us, she would be safe here. We would know where she was and could protect her."

Charles turned away from his father in frustration. He understood why he did what he did, but still it made him angry that he hadn't known sooner. He could have prevented her from leaving. Now he had to figure out a way to rescue her if she did not return. Then he would have to explain to them about Blackstone's involvement with Shears.

He walked to the window, hoping to see the carriage return her to their safety, but the roadway was empty. It was getting dark. If he left for the Blackstones' house now, it would look strange that he was following the hired help. Also, it would reveal her cover. Blackstone would discover who she was and wouldn't think twice about getting rid of that loose end. She was one of the few individuals who could link Blackstone to Shears.

Blackstone was playing a tricky game. He portrayed himself as a strong supporter of the Crown, but in truth, he was in line with its number one enemy. He could not let his family know this. It put them into too much danger.

He pulled out his pocket watch and noted the time. He would give her half an hour to return. That gave her plenty of time to deliver the message. He slid the timepiece back into his pocket and turned toward his family.

"Were there any more errands?" Charles asked Ivy.

Ivy shook her head in denial. "I would never have sent her if I had known who she was."

Charles went over to Ivy and grabbed her hands in his. He squeezed them lightly. "I know. She had us fooled."

"What is your plan?" Thorn inquired.

"I will give her time to return. If she doesn't come back soon, I will have to look for her. When she returns, I ask you to give me time alone with her."

Thorn nodded his head in acceptance.

"I will try to convince her to go to Margate with you. I will need you to watch over her while I finish my business in town."

"We will take care of her at Thornhill Manor."

Charles released Ivy's hands and walked back over to the window. He pulled the shades back and watched as darkness engulfed the sky, casting shadows along the street. His fingers tapped impatiently on the windowsill as he waited for her to return.

"Let us finish with our packing, dear. We need to leave as soon as she arrives." Thorn drew Ivy out of the room.

"I am sorry, son."

"There is nothing to be sorry for, Father."

"If that is the case, then why are you sending her to Thornhill Manor and not to our home?"

"Because I want you to stay at Thornhill too until I can get the proper security in place."

"Nonsense. We have adequate security in place at Mallton Manor."

"Humor me, Father. Please stay with the Thornhills until I can return home."

The duke let out a sigh, resigned that it was the least he could do. His son was under tremendous pressure, and he did not need to add to it. This way he could spend more time with Ivy and Tommy. The boy made him feel young again. More than that, he made him feel needed.

He rose from his chair, walked over to Charles, and put his hand on his shoulder.

"I am going to the townhome. Send word when your Raina has returned. I will be ready to make the journey back home. All will be well, my son. Have faith."

"I am trying, Father," he said as he continued to wait for Raina to return.

Chapter Nine

RAINA LET HERSELF IN through the servant's entrance. As with the rest of the house, it was shrouded in darkness. She had waited in the mews behind the house for a sign the family had settled for the night. She had watched while the guards searched the house looking for her. Raina felt awful that the Thornhills were objected to that. When the guards had left, she sat in wait, needing to gather her things and leave as quick as she could. She made her way up the servant's staircase to her room. Not wanting to awaken anybody, she guided her way through the darkness with the touch of her hands.

When she was first hired on, she did an intense scrutiny of the residence. She found every exit and hiding place she could use for just these circumstances. As she climbed the stairs, she moved up them, zigzagging her way over the creaks she knew they made. When she came to the floor of her room, she opened the door quietly, easing herself onto the landing. As she closed the door behind her, she relaxed when she saw the hallway covered in darkness. There were no lights peeking out from underneath the closed bedroom doors.

Silently she crept along the hallway to her room. As she opened the door, she slid inside her bedroom. She leaned back against the closed door, shutting her eyes and breathing a sigh of relief. She moved to the wardrobe. She needed to put as much distance between herself and London as soon as possible. Now she was a wanted woman she must change her appearance once more. She had to leave before anyone awoke and caught her.

Her hand swept the bottom of the wardrobe, searching for her valise, but the bottom was empty. She dropped to her knees as she continued to search the darkness, her hands brushing in between the dresses that hung. She panicked. Where was it? Did they figure out who she was?

She searched on her knees, crawling around the wardrobe. Maybe one of the maids had moved it. While she searched on her hands and knees around the floor of the dresser, her body tensed. She was not alone. She was off her game. Her instincts did not notice the uninvited guest when she first came into the room.

Reaching into her boot, she drew out her small knife and slid it into the pocket of her dress. She didn't know who her visitor was, but she wanted to be prepared. But in case it was Tommy, she did not want to scare the boy. Drawing herself to her feet, she smoothed out her dress and pretended that she was unaware of her visitor. She walked over to the side of the bed to light her lantern.

"Do not light that, Raina—or shall I say Mrs. Whitlow?" She heard the sarcasm in his voice.

She turned slowly at the sound of his voice that had been occupying her thoughts. He was sitting in the rocking chair, rocking back and forth. The light from the firelight showed her valise resting on his lap. His hand was slid through the handle, with his fingers tapping a tattoo on the bag. Well, she'd found her missing bag at least. To get it from his hands and leave without him following her was going be another difficult task. This time she didn't think she could accomplish that mission.

She wanted to answer the sarcasm in his voice with her own but couldn't. Raina felt defeated as she sat on the edge of the bed. She didn't want to fight him. The past few months had taken their toll on her emotions. After what she had been through tonight, she was at her breaking point. But because of tonight, she also realized she wasn't finished. That was taken out of her hands. Now more than ever, she must run. But this time she was not going to run to her next step to destroying Shears. She was running to save her own life.

She had to disappear and hide where nobody could find her. Charles was another obstacle she had to get through tonight. She has managed to avoid him and get out of his clutches before, so tonight would be no different.

"Are you going somewhere, Mallory?"

"Yes, as a matter of fact. We are."

Raina laughed. "We?"

"Yes, you and I are leaving here tonight. Together," Charles emphasized.

"I am not going anywhere with you," Raina argued.

"Well, you made that possible tonight, didn't you?"

"I did not cause his death," Raina said, defended herself.

"That is not what the authorities think. They even seem to know you are Raina LeClair, not Mrs. Whitlow. How do you think they learned that?"

"He was already dead when I got there."

Charles watched her. He saw the panic in her eyes. Also the fear. When he discovered the details on how Blackstone had died, he knew she was not capable of the murder. This had Shears written all over it. It was a perfect way to get rid of two of his loose ends. Only he wouldn't get rid of this loose end. Charles would make sure of that.

Charles patted her valise. "I assume that you already have your next disguise ready to go."

Raina nodded. They had her trapped. She had no way out of London, let alone England, without his help. She would go along with his plans until she could make her escape. Then she would disappear from England and him, where they would never find her.

As he rose from the chair, Charles walked over and set the valise on the bed next to her. He then returned to sit back in his seat.

"I will give you ten minutes to change and to gather all your belongings. But then it shouldn't take you that long, considering you already had your luggage ready to run."

Raina ignored the sarcasm in his words as she opened her valise. She pulled out her disguise and laid the pieces on the bed.

"May I have a few moments of privacy to change?"

"No, you may not. Do you think for one minute I will let you out of my sight?"

"Will you at least be a gentleman and turn around?"

"I ceased being a gentleman to you when you drugged me."

Raina paled at his words, realizing that he learned she was the tavern wench. If he knew of that disguise, then he probably recognized all the others. If he didn't know of her different disguises, then it might be easier to get away from him than she thought.

She realized she was sloppy on her Mrs. Whitlow disguise. There were key times she fell out of her role as an old companion. His arrival at the Thornhills' shook her up more than she thought. It was her own fault she had been discovered. She needed to get her head in the game and focus.

She turned her back on him and began to disrobe. There was nowhere else to hide. Even though she had been put in the same wing as her employers, she still had a servant's quarters. She was only on this floor to be near Tommy. There were no dressing screens to change behind. She would have to change in front of him.

Raina had made her disguises accessible to change swiftly for just these emergencies. Unbuttoning a few buttons to loosen the top of her dress, she pulled the dress up over her head. The garment became caught in the pins holding her wig on her head. As she struggled to undo her dress, she heard chuckling behind her. Gritting her teeth, she disentangled the dress from her hair. With the wig half on, she undid the pins and pulled it off her head.

Laying the pins on the table next to the bed, she ran her fingers through her hair. Her fingers massaged her scalp, easing the tightness from having her hair pulled tight all day. She untangled her long black hair with her fingers.

She looked over her shoulder to glare at Charles for laughing at her and paused, her hands falling from her hair. Her eyes were captured in his gaze, every single one of her thoughts forgotten at his look.

Charles fingers gripped the arm rests tighter. The sight of her was a punch in the gut. She was amazingly gorgeous. He never seen another lady look as incredible as she did at this moment. With her long black hair hanging to the middle of her back, he was lost. He wished it was his hands stroking through her hair.

But it wasn't only her hair that stopped him from laughing, it was the creamy white skin of her shoulder illuminated in the firelight, begging for his kiss. He could imagine himself kissing the spot where her neck curved into her shoulder, his lips drawing a trail across her body. She stood looking at him in only in her chemise, with her dark blue eyes turning to midnight at his gaze.

When he saw that she had realized where his thoughts had turned, he rose from the chair and pulled her into his arms.

He lowered his head and ravished her mouth with his, drawing on every emotion he had felt as he waited for her this afternoon. He suffered through too many to even recognize what he was experiencing anymore. All he knew was what he was feeling at this moment. Desire.

He listened to her gasp as he caught her unaware. Stealing this moment, he slid his tongue into her mouth and stroked it alongside hers. Fast, urgent, he stroked her tongue.

He pulled her body in closer to his, holding her to him as tight as he could. Charles needed the reassurance she was real and not a figment of his imagination. He had been searching for her for far too long. There were always obstacles in their way, herself the major one.

Pulling his mouth away from her lips, he drew his lips down her neck to the spot he craved to kiss. His tongue slid along the curve, tasting her sweetness. Drawing out the sensation, he blew a soft breath where he had licked. He felt her shiver in his arms.

His lips sank into the curve as he kissed her slowly. His lips blazed a trail of fire from her shoulder to her neck. He could feel the heat coming off her body. Bending backward, he lay her body across the bed. As he followed down next to her, his mouth never left her body.

Charles untied her chemise when he heard no arguments about his kisses. His lips worked their way from her shoulder to the top of her breasts. He trailed the top of the ribbon across the opening, placing little kisses along the path. Opening the chemise wider, he saw the outline of her breasts. The soft globes begging for his lips.

Lowering his lips to the curve of her breasts, he placed featherlight kisses along the slope. Hearing her moan, he repeated on the other breast. Wanting more, he undid the ribbon, pulling her chemise completely open.

He looked up for her reaction and saw desire darken her eyes to almost black. When he realized there would be no rejection, he lowered his head to taste the sweet buds that were beckoning to him. Drawing one into his mouth, he savored the sweetness of Raina. Charles moaned as he sucked her nipple between his lips, drawing out every drop of honey that was her. When he felt her nipple tighten inside his mouth, he softly circled his tongue around her bud.

When her hands ran throughout his hair, it was the encouragement he needed. He traced a path across to her other breast with his tongue. Repeating the love on her other breast, his hands roamed the rest of her body. He wanted to touch her everywhere. His hands glided over her curves, pulling her body in closer to him.

No matter how close he drew her in, he needed her closer. He wanted her to be the other half of him. But he couldn't get enough. He was drowning in the taste and touch of her. Even though he could see her touching him and responding to his touch, he knew she was holding herself back from him. While he was pulling her close, she was resisting.

He wanted her completely, and he wanted her as undone as he was. For he was undone. Having her in his arms, kissing her, touching her was unraveling him to no end.

Raina recognized she was losing the last of her control. As hard as she was trying to hold on, she saw herself slipping with every touch and a kiss from him. She lost her senses, except for the sense of feel. She wanted to experience everything where Charles was concerned.

As she ran her fingers through his thick hair, she held him to her breasts. Her body was on fire while she was with him, and his kisses enflamed her more. Every lick of his tongue or nip of his lips tightened her nipples harder. She arched her body into him, craving more.

When he moved his hand up her legs underneath her chemise, she knew she had to put a stop to this. It was too dangerous of a game to play with him, and Raina knew she would come out the loser.

But when his hand slid between her thighs, coaxing her legs to open wider, Raina knew she couldn't end this now. As her thighs parted for him, her body overruled her mind and wanted to continue to play.

Charles left her breasts and made a path back up to her lips. He slid his tongue across her lips as his fingers caressed her wetness. Raina moaned against his lips.

"Charles, you must stop."

"Just one touch, Raina," Charles begged.

Raina moaned as his fingers explored. She knew she must halt this madness.

Charles took the moan as encouragement. Sliding his tongue into her mouth, he kissed her passionately. When she returned his kiss with the stroke of her tongue, that was all he needed.

He slid his finger inside her, her wetness coating his finger like honey. Raina pulled her mouth from his, gasping at his touch. Watching her, he saw the flame of desire in her eyes turn into the passion he was feeling for her. This feeling went beyond any feeling of craving, but one of a passionate need that only she could fulfill, no other. He saw in her eyes that she had the same need for him that he held for her.

Setting a rhythm with his finger, he drove her passion higher, wanting her to come fully undone. Her resistance was fading away. He could feel it in every stroke of his finger. Sliding in and out of her wetness, he sensed her quivering with an unmistakable need.

He knew he had her when she wrapped her arms around him and pulled his head toward her for a kiss. It wasn't just any kiss. It was a kiss from a woman surrendering to passion. A kiss that showed him what she was feeling.

Raina kissed Charles with the pent-up emotions she had been suffering with these last few months. The need she had for him to make herself feel complete. When her hands ran through his hair, it was all the encouragement he needed.

Their lips molding into one, caressing one another as their tongues stroked the fire even hotter. Raina placed little kisses along his lip, along the way gently sucking his lower lip into her mouth. Then, just as quickly, her tongue stroked his, tasting him. Wanting more from him.

She sensed her body was going to explode.

Charles felt her losing control. He wanted her to explode in his arms. His thumb began to stroke her clit as he slid in another finger deep into her wetness. He set up a rhythm, stroking her. He noticed her unraveling. Flicking his thumb back and forth quicker, she tightened around his fingers.

Raina grasped onto Charles tighter. She felt like she was being engulfed in flames. Her fingers dug into his back as he brought her to such heights. She didn't understand what was happening to her body. She only knew she did not want him to stop. It was ecstasy.

"Let go, sweet Raina, let go," Charles whispered in her ear.

He began to suck the very same spot of her neck where it all started moments ago, his fingers softly stroking her higher as his mouth breathed fire onto her body. He felt her body shake as it lost control. Smiling into her shoulder, his fingers brought her body to fulfillment.

As her body arched into his hand, he could feel the wetness coating it. He kissed her deeply, drawing out her gasp into his mouth at her surrender.

Her body had surrendered to his touch. Now he only needed her heart to do the same.

Chapter Ten

HER HEART HAD FINALLY surrendered to him, but she would not allow him to know that. One touch from him had brought down every single one of her defenses. She closed her eyes as she felt him pull away from her body. He did not move far from her. She still enjoyed the heat of him caressing her. She could sense him watching her, as he waited for her to respond to him.

How was she to react when she didn't how to respond to herself? Her mind was a jumble of incomplete thoughts she did not want to understand. She only wanted to feel. Feel him. Every inch of him against her. She was tired of thinking and planning, but most of all, she was tired of running.

What would it hurt? To just feel. To savor the touch and taste of the man she loved. What if she were to reach out and touch him the way he touched her? To place her lips on his body the same way he enjoyed her? To let herself be loved and to show her love?

Opening her eyes, she saw him gazing at her. He lay with his hand propping up his head. His dark emerald eyes were watching for her reaction to him. Waiting.

Her eyes dropped to his lips. They were parted as if they were waiting patiently for her lips to lay claim to them. She reached her hand up to his face. Her fingers brushed faintly across his lips. They were soft and smooth to her touch. Sliding her hand across his cheek, she felt the soft bristles of his beard scrape her hand.

He had not shaved this evening. It looked primitive to her. Her hand continued to slide into the thick tresses of his golden hair. As her hand brought his head forward to hers, she rose to meet his lips.

Raina placed her lips on his parted lips and kissed him. She could hear his groan at her advancement. But he held back.

She kissed him tenderly, exploring his mouth with her lips. Soft, slow, gentle kisses savoring the flavor of him. She slid her tongue inside his mouth, tasting him fully, gliding her tongue along his, slowly skimming her tongue across his lips.

Raising her eyes up to his, she saw the reaction she was having on him. His eyes turned a darker green. She saw the raw desire in them.

Her kisses moved to his neck as her hands found the buttons on his shirt. Her fingers shook, not from fear, but from desire. The tiny studs came apart like magic at her touch.

Peeling his shirt open with her fingers, she touched his bare chest. He lay as still as he could be for her while her hands explored him. She felt his muscles tense as her hands roamed over his body. He was rock hard. There was not a part of him soft to her touch. Raina decided that she needed to taste him too. Her lips kissed a path from his neck to his chest, following the dips of his muscled body.

Raina's fingers encountered his bandage. Charles hissed in pain and Raina drew back, looking at him in fear. He shook his head at her and brought her fingers back to his injuries. Softly pressing her fingers to his ribs, he closed his eyes at her gentle touch. She wanted to heal him with all her need. She replaced her fingers with her lips. As she kissed him with her lips, she could feel his body relaxing into hers.

Raina sensed the pain leaving his body at her touch. Without even realizing it, tears slid from her face and settled on his wounds. She could taste them as she kissed him.

He felt her tears against her kisses. Pulling her up his body, he wrapped her in his arms. He slid his thumbs across her cheeks and saw the tears as they slid along his hand. As he gazed into her eyes, he saw her pain.

"Oh, Raina. Don't cry for me, sweetheart," Charles whispered.

"If not for me, you wouldn't be hurt."

"Shh," he whispered.

As he bent his head, he captured her next words into his mouth, drawing out her hurt and pain into himself. Their kisses were soft and cautious, each one holding back from letting their true passions explode. They both were vulnerable to one another.

Pulling back, he looked into her eyes. He knew it was time to stop this before his desire was out of his control. They didn't have time to explore their passion, nor was this the place.

"We need to leave here, Raina. It is not safe."

"I will leave. You stay with your family."

"I will not leave you alone," Charles argued.

"You will be in more danger alongside me. I can escape better without you trailing along with me."

Charles laughed. "You don't think I can change into a disguise any better than you?"

Raina pulled back at his laughter toward her. Her feelings were hurt when he didn't take her concerns seriously. Pulling her chemise closed, she laced the ribbons back together, tying it together in a small bow. As she rose from the bed, she dug in her valise for her disguise.

Lifting her chin, she glared at him. "No, I don't think you can, my lord."

Raina baited him with his title. She knew it would rankle him. For that was what he was. A titled aristocrat playing at spy. He did not know how to play at the serious game they involved themselves in. It was obvious at the injuries that his body kept acquiring.

Charles rubbed his hands together. "Mmm, that sounds like a challenge, sweet Raina."

Raina continued glaring at him, becoming frustrated at his lack of concern for their predicament. Shaking her head and rolling her eyes, she dug out her costume and got ready to leave. She needed to put as much distance between herself and London as soon as possible. Their little interlude did not help her with her time constraint.

Pausing, she reflected on their passion, filing the memories away into her heart before she left him again. As she looked at him, she did not regret what they shared but cherished the feelings he made her experience. She smiled wistfully and began to dress.

Putting on her costume entailed cosmetic alteration. The clothes were simple, but the rest of the disguise needed extra work. She needed to make herself look as plain as possible, but without drawing too much attention to her plainness. While she could not look too ugly for people to notice, she did not want her true beauty to shine either. Raina was not a vain woman, but she knew she was stunning. It garnered her an abundance of unwanted attention as she grew into a woman, but she never used that to her advantage. Ever since she could remember, she had to alter her image so she never got the power to use it to her full potential. Not that she wanted to. Her beauty did not define who she was or what she felt.

As she pulled on the maid uniform and the plain, pale-brown stockings, she sensed she was alone. When her eyes scanned the room, she saw that Charles had disappeared. When she glanced toward the door, she saw it was still closed. Where did he go? How did she not hear him leave?

Making her way to the door, she opened it and viewed the length of the hallway. It was shrouded in darkness. There was no sign of him. She noticed the door to his room was closed, and no light shone underneath the door. She closed the door and made her way back to her bag and finished with her disguise.

She took out the pale-brown wig and set to pulling her long black hair into a bun. She slipped the wig over the bun and secured it tightly to her hair with pins. After she finished with her hair, she set to work on her makeup. She'd have to do this in the dark.

She understood why Charles did not want her to light the candle. The house was under surveillance. She saw the guards before she snuck into the house. Now she had to find a way to avoid them when she took her leave.

After putting the finishing touches to her disguise, she sat and laced the standard black shoes she saw the maids wear. As she walked back and forth across her room to get her feet used to them, she grimaced. Those poor girls had to wear such uncomfortable footwear. She practiced the unhurried walk of a maid, emerging herself into her new role. She practiced the mannerisms for a short while, for she could not make a single error outside of this room. If she was to stay alive, she must be believable.

Once she realized she was ready, she closed the valise and began to exit the room. She stopped at the brief knock on her door. Frozen, she stood still. If she didn't answer, she ran the risk of the intruder coming inside. But if she did respond, who did she answer as, Mrs. Whitlow or Daisy the upstairs maid?

It was taken out of her control when the door opened. Expecting it to be Charles, she was surprised to see Ivy Thornhill standing there.

Caught unaware, Raina waited for Ivy to speak first. She waited as Ivy closed the door and advanced toward her. Sitting the valise on the floor, Raina folded her hands in front of her.

Ivy surprised her when she laid her hands over hers and squeezed gently.

"You don't have to speak a word. I can only imagine the horror you have been living the last few months. I want you to understand that you have our family's full support."

Tears came to Raina's eyes at Ivy's kind words. She was not expecting this. She thought they would be angry at her for bringing danger to their front door. Why was she so sentimental tonight? Every action toward her was touching on emotions she thought she had buried deep inside herself. It was not time for reflection; she needed to leave. Sincere as Ivy was toward her, Raina knew better. She knew Thorn had nothing but contempt for her and was angry at everything she put his family through.

"Your husband doesn't feel the same way."

"That is where you are wrong, Raina. May I call you Raina?"

"I am Daisy, my lady," Raina replied as she dropped into a curtsey.

Ivy frowned at her stubbornness. In time she would win her over. Of course, now was not the time. But before she let Raina escape again, she would offer her friendship.

"Please let me aid you in your escape."

Raina nodded her head, too choked to speak.

This was too much. Raina had to get out of there before she let her fear overtake her. She was too vulnerable.

"It is time for you to leave. Come quickly." Ivy rushed Raina toward the door.

Raina trailed Ivy. They walked down the stairs and made their way to the kitchen.

"Please allow John to accompany you out of England."

"I cannot let your servant endanger his life."

"It will draw less suspicion if you leave with another servant."

Raina knew Ivy was correct. If two servants were perceived sneaking away tonight, no words would be spoken. But if she were to leave on her own, they would know it was her.

Raina looked John over; he looked similar to the servants employed by the Thornhills, but she did not recognize him. Maybe he worked in the stables. It looked like he visited the kitchen a lot.

He could pass as her father, though a little on the plump side. For the sideburns on his face were white, peppered with black hair. He pulled his cap off at her inquiry, his balding pate shining brightly in the candlelight. Glasses covered his eyes, and he smiled kindly at her. He was stooped over, his hand gripping the cane by his side. She could see his hand shake slightly and frowned. How was this kind old man to save her if they encountered danger?

Ivy opened the door and spoke loud enough for the guards to hear her.

"Daisy, I hope you and your father make it home safe to your mother. Take every bit of time you need in helping your family. Your position will still be available upon your return."

Raina went into a curtsy. "Thank you, my lady, for your kind understanding," Raina spoke in a quiet, timid voice.

She watched as John twisted his cap in his hand as he addressed Ivy.

"Thank you, my lady, for letting our Daisy come nurse her mama to better health." He spoke in a northerly accent.

"Godspeed on your journey home."

Ivy closed the door behind them. Raina followed John to the cart hitched out in front of the Thornhills' townhome. He helped her into the cart and leaned on his cane as he walked around to the other side. When he stopped at the horses he whispered to them, holding out his hand to give them a treat.

"You over there, help an old man into his cart," John yelled over at the patrol standing guard over the Thornhill home.

Raina tensed in her seat, gripping her valise. Why was he drawing unwanted attention their way? Did Lady Thornhill not give him any insight into their danger?

"Papa, you can manage fine on your own," Raina said, trying to encourage John to climb into the carriage.

"Nonsense, my dear. My hip won't allow it. These boys can help us on our way."

Raina watched in fear as the guards walked over to John to help him up into the cart. They glimpsed at her for a brief moment and decided she was too plain to take any notice of. When they ignored her, Raina breathed a short sigh of relief that her disguise worked.

"Thank you, boys. What are you standing around here for anyway? If you don't mind me asking?"

"We are looking for a murderer. You best be on your way and get your daughter to safety."

"That I will do. Good evening," John answered and clicked at the horses to be on their way.

Raina looked over her shoulder as the cart made its way along the cobblestone street. The guards were turned around and were watching the Thornhill residence for any sign of Raina LeClair, aka Mrs. Whitlow, to make an appearance. Little did they know she came and left as young Daisy, the maid who was returning home to nurse her sick mother. Relaxing in the seat, she sat back and closed her eyes. The last couple of days had taken their toll on her. Her body swayed with the movement of the cart, lulling her into sleep. She would rest for a few moments, and then she would persuade John to let her off at the first inn they reach outside of London. Then Daisy would no longer be.

~~~~~~~

The room was littered with empty bottles and discarded food. That was nothing compared to the stench filling the office. Smoke filled the air as the man at the desk puffed away on a cigar. His scuffed boots propped on the desk as he slouched in his chair. He listened as his messenger tried to explain to him that the girl had vanished. *Vanished my ass*, he thought.

"I swear on me mother's grave that she is gone," the young lad explained as he shuffled closer to the door. He saw the anger boiling in the captain's eyes. He drew the short straw and was tasked with giving him the awful news. He wanted to be as far from this office that his legs could take him.

The captain kicked his feet from the desk and stood. He ground out his cigar on the desk, throwing the stub on the floor with the others. He leaned his hands on the desk and glared at the boy.

"What do you mean that she is gone? Where did she go?"

Grabbing the door, he was ready to make a run for it as he explained.

"Your contact in the house said she left a few days ago. But we have been watching the house, sir, and the only one that has left is a maid named Daisy. She left with her father to take care of her mum, who is real sick."

The captain came around the desk and grabbed the boy by his shirt, lifting him up to his face, and shook him.

"You stupid imbecile, Raina LeClair was the girl and Mallory was her father. Where did they go?"

"I don't know, Captain," the boy stuttered out.

Shears threw the boy up against the wall and dropped him.

"Worthless, the whole lot of you are. Get out."

The boy ran from the room. Shears kicked the door shut and went back to his desk. Opening his drawer, he pulled out a new cigar. As he lit the cigar, he watched as the man came out of the shadows and advanced toward him.

"Bring her to me, and I will consider your debt paid," Shears offered.

"Mallory will not let that piece out of his sight."

"Kill him. Better yet, kill her."

"I am not a murderer."

"Aren't you?"

"If I do this for you, you will give me the information I seek?"

"Better yet, I will take you to it, my lord."

The man nodded and left the office.

Shears leaned back in his chair and drew a long drag on the cigar. He laughed to himself at how easy he could manipulate people. Everybody did his bidding for the right price. And he always made sure he had the prize for everyone who did his bidding. He wouldn't release this prize though; the outcome was much grander. Actually, he would not have to give it up in the end, because he would make sure every single enemy of his paid.

Chapter Eleven

STRETCHING HER ACHING MUSCLES, Raina struggled to awaken. Her body ached in places she never realized could hurt. She fought the last of sleep and opened her eyes to quiet. It wasn't exactly quiet; she could hear birds chirping their morning melodies. Except for the sounds of nature, she could hear no other noises. No horses clopping along the street, no street vendors selling their wares, no sounds of servants scurrying around as they performed their daily chores.

As she glanced around, she noticed the simplicity of the room. It was a good size room for an inn, for the use of the aristocracy traveling through to their destinations. Whoever owned this inn went to no expense to the comfort of their guests. The walls were decorated with green paint, nothing too masculine but exactly the right shade for men and women. As she observed the room, she noted the furniture catered to both sexes. Lighter pieces for the women to relax in with more dominant pieces for the men. Overall, it was a cozy room. Raina felt herself relaxing until she realized she didn't understand how she arrived there.

She closed her eyes and tried to recall when they arrived at the inn. But the only thing she remembered was shutting her eyes for a spell after they departed the Thornhills'. After that she could not recollect anything. How did she arrive in this room? Where was she?

Feeling a slight movement on the bed, Raina opened her eyes. She never moved. So, who lay next to her in the bed? As she turned her head to the side, she saw John lying next to her, still deep in sleep. Her eyes widened at the audacity of the servant. How dare he lay in bed with her? Who did he think he was? She needed to remove herself from this bed and leave this room now.

Gently lifting the cover off her body, she started to move off the bed—quietly so not to awaken John. She felt the rush of cool air hit her bare body. Raina gasped as she realized she was only clad in her chemise and that the rest of her body was bare. This angered her. How dare he? He went too far. Raina was about to let out her rage when his arm flung across her body and pulled her into his embrace.

She stiffened. She needed to find a way out before he awoke. This was entirely improper. Not that she was a proper miss, with her exploits these last few months. She didn't want to be violated. To think Lady Ivy thought this servant could be trusted.

When she saw John relax against her in sleep again, she eased away. As soon as she was out of his grasp, he pulled her in again and mumbled in his sleep. Raina could not actually understand the words. Something about being an ungrateful miss disturbing his sleep.

Raina's body moved still again, and she counted to one hundred. She hoped it would be enough time and that he would roll away from her. She wanted to scream but didn't want to draw any untoward attention to them. She couldn't afford to be caught by any servants. The fewer people who remembered her being there, the better. She didn't want anyone to be able to track her whereabouts after she left.

As she lay there counting, John still had not relaxed his hold on her. If anything, he tightened his grip, pulling her closer. Her body pressed tightly against his, making her very aware of his body. Raina panicked, and her breathing quickened as she struggled to grasp the realization she was going to be accosted.

Raina put her hands on his chest and tried to push herself out of his hold. His chest vibrated with laughter. Confused, she looked up and saw the amusement twinkling in his eyes. Eyes that were the color of emeralds. The exact eyes of the gentleman who was constantly in her thoughts. It was when she noticed his smug smile that she realized he had fooled her.

She shook her head. How did she not see the signs of his disguise? She had been too caught up in her getaway to realize every player in the game. This only proved she needed to disappear from England and start a new life. She had lost her edge. Her father would have been so disappointed in her. He had trained her better than this.

Charles had known he needed to take pity on her. It had gone on long enough. He was just hoping for a few moments of shut-eye. He had driven them through the night to get as far from London as possible, only stopping once to change the horses. During the night, Raina never woke once. He realized she was exhausted. He hadn't expected the charade to last so long. After they left London behind, he was going to expose himself. But she had laid her head on his shoulder in sleep before they had even left the city limits.

Her body relaxed for the whole ride to the cottage. When she still had not awoken, he carried her into bed and collapsed beside her. Exhaustion had taken a toll on him too. The jarring wagon on his battered body did not help either. So, he held her to him and fell asleep with her in his arms.

Charles noticed the moment she woke. He regarded her from behind lowered lids. She had looked relaxed in the quiet environment, but he saw the moment she planned her escape. Just as she was doing now. Little did she know he would do everything in his power to hold her here. She was not going anywhere.

"Where are you going, missy?" Charles kept to his disguised voice.

"I am not your missy, and you may let go of me now, Charles Mallory," Raina stated as she tried to pull away.

"Never," Raina thought she heard him whisper.

He pulled her in closer and nuzzled her neck. If a lady's body was able to relax and stiffen at the same moment, Raina's did. He sensed she was enjoying his kisses, but her body was still in flight mode.

He knew he should not seduce her. She was too vulnerable. He needed her to trust him, and taking advantage of her now would not make her trust him. So, he gathered her close and just held her. To have her close and safe in his arms was all he needed for now.

"Relax, Raina. I only want to hold you. You are safe here with me."

"Where are we?" Her voice was muffled against his chest.

"At a cottage that belongs to my father."

"Where?"

"Where is not important. We will not be discovered here. Nobody knows of this place. It will be a safe place to hide until we depart."

"Where?" Raina asked again.

Charles pulled back from her and tipped her chin up to look into her eyes. He wanted her to understand how serious he was in keeping her at the cottage, safe from London and from Shears.

"I am not telling you where we are so you can escape from me again. I am here to protect you from Shears, and we shall come up with a plan to end him. But we must plot together on this, not apart. Do you understand?"

"I work alone, Mallory."

"Not this time."

Raina pinched her lips, displeased at his words. Charles sensed he needed to coax her into agreeing to his plans. He ran his thumb across her lips, smoothing them out before bringing his lips to hers. He tenderly kissed them open, exploring her mouth with gentle kisses. Letting his mouth show her she was safe with him. Whisper-like kisses adorned her lips. He heard her sigh and realized she was releasing her hold on her emotions. Deepening the kiss, he let her know he would never leave her side again.

Raina sensed his promises in his kiss and wanted to believe him. She didn't know how to place her trust with anybody, but his kisses guided her to trust him. She wanted to believe in him. Maybe in trusting her body's reaction to him, she could learn to trust her heart with him too. She decided to work with him and opened herself to the kiss.

Charles sensed the change in her. He let her control the kiss, keeping a hold on his passion. Her lips were smooth as she brushed her lips across his. The flavor of her honeyed lips enflamed his desire for more. Holding himself back from exploring her vulnerable body was becoming more difficult. As much as he wanted to lie in bed the entire day and hold her, he needed to put distance between them until she was ready. He would not take advantage of her and confuse her.

He needed to show her she could trust him, and he wanted more from her than this. Charles wanted to build a life with her. If she learned of his plan, she would run as far and fast as she could. He had to show her they were meant to be.

Raina could see Charles pulling back from her. Did she misread his signals? She knew he wanted her; she felt him pressed against her hip. Why was he holding back? Raina wasn't a simple miss; she recognized when a man was aroused. She has seen it all in her adventures. Charles Mallory was most definitely a man who wanted her. So why was he putting distance between them? Maybe she had misunderstood him and he only wanted to help her, not a relationship with her. Oh, he wanted a relationship, just one of the sensual sense and not one of the marriageable sense. Raina should have known better. She was not his type, and she didn't come from a proper family. He apparently needed to marry a demure lady of peerage. Not a spy's daughter.

Could Raina have a sexual relationship with him? Could she give over her body and heart to a man who could not give his back in return? Raina decided yes. She would take this time and refocus on her mission. During that time, she would give into her feelings for Charles and store the memories away for a time to reflect on later.

Realizing what she wanted now, she became the aggressor. She would not allow him time to think, but to enjoy. To love her touch and need for him.

Raina shifted her body against his innocently. Charles bit back a groan. She was driving him crazy. He was trying to do the right, upstanding, gentlemanly thing, but she was making it impossible for him.

When she snuggled into his chest and slid her hand inside his shirt, he was done for. He tilted his head back, gritting his teeth in pure agony. He didn't realize she had unbuttoned his shirt because he was so focused on keeping his arousal in check. As her hands spread his shirt apart, he nearly jumped from the bed when her lips made contact with his chest. Soft butterfly kisses across his torso.

He slid his head forward and saw her watching him as she kissed him. She was waiting for his reaction. When he didn't respond, she moved up his body, kissing him along the way. Her featherlight kisses grazed across his chest to settle on his neck. When her tongue darted out between her lips to lick his neck, it was the end of his patience.

"Raina," he growled before he took her mouth under his and kissed her. He hungered for the taste and touch of her.

His kiss dominated her senses, and she wanted him with the same need. She matched his kisses, a kiss for a kiss. His hands slid into her long, raven hair and tilted her head back to kiss her more deeply. He couldn't get enough of her and only wanted more. The need for her was stronger than anything he had ever experienced in his life.

Charles needed to touch her as desperately as he needed to kiss her. His hands lowered and brought her chemise off her body in one final sweep, their lips only parting enough for the fabric to slip past their hunger. His hands pulled her up against his body, sinking into her delicate flesh. They roamed her body, as if they knew the direction to go. She was so soft. And warm.

Charles tore his lips from hers and pulled back. He needed to see her. Every inch of her. She was exquisite. Her eyes were closed, her lips parted and swollen from their kisses. His eyes wandered down, watching her breasts as they rose in rhythm to her breathing. Her nipples were tight buds waiting for his lips. He brushed his thumb across one, watching as her eyes opened, and she gasped. He repeated on her other nipple. Watching them tighten more, he continued. Her breasts continued to rise up and down from her deep breaths.

Extending his gaze, he moved his eyes to her stomach and the curve of her hips. Raina was not like those silly debutantes or ladies of the ton. Her body was curvaceous in all the right places. She filled out a man's hand, making him ache for more.

As his eyes moved lower, he could see the wetness glistening off her curls. He closed his eyes and moaned. Opening them again, he finished the journey down the length of her long legs. Legs that he wanted to wrap around his hips as he drove into her over and over. From what he glimpsed of her last night, it was nothing to seeing her in the daylight. Every delectable bit of her.

He slid his hand down and gently brought it up her leg. His fingers trailed up the smooth expanse of her legs and over her knees, moving higher. Her legs were pressed tightly together. As he traced his finger between her thighs, they parted for him.

Her wetness glistened in the sunlight shining through the window, begging for his touch. He wanted to sink into her now. His cock throbbed at the sight of her, but he knew she wasn't ready for him. If he even touched her there now, he could not hold back any longer. He had to slow down.

He slid his hand up over her wetness and across her stomach, making his way back up to her breasts. He heard her moan as if in protest. Then he lifted her breasts into his hands with his thumbs, stroking her nipples, which enticed a different moan from her. Smiling, he lowered his head to take the pink-tipped nipples into his mouth.

Softly biting them, he lavished them with his tongue. When he felt her fingers running through his hair and holding his head to her breasts tighter, he knew what she wanted. He sucked harder on her nipple, pulling out her desires. Making her come undone in his arms. He wanted her wild for him. Wanted her to unravel her soul in his arms.

Her hands held his head tightly to her breasts. She wanted more. She didn't know what more consisted of, but she wanted him to ease the ache building in her body. She had to touch him. Wanting to touch his body against her made Raina desperate. Pulling at his shirt, she pulled it up, wanting it off his body. Charles sensed her need and pulled away from her, lifting the shirt over his head and throwing it across the room. She watched as he continued to get rid of the rest of his clothes.

She did not take her eyes off him as he stripped his pants off his legs. Her eyes devoured him. The bruising on his body made him no less of a man. They intensified the muscles that shaped him. She wanted to kiss and touch every injury on him and heal him with her love. When she saw his arousal for her, she wanted to touch him. Reaching out to touch his hardness, he stopped her hand with his.

Raina raised her eyes to his in question.

"Raina, if you touch me, I won't be able to stop," he tried to explain.

"I don't want you to stop."

"Tell me you want me as desperately as I want you."

Raina raised up on her knees and ran her hands across the muscles she admired. As she pulled his head to hers, she whispered, "I not only want you, but I need you."

Her touch and kiss, but most of all her words undid him. He pulled her to him and kissed her as he slid her body underneath him. His hands went to part her thighs but found them open for him, waiting for his touch. He slid his finger inside her, sinking into her wetness. When she clenched around his finger, he knew she was ready for him.

Pulling away from her kiss, he rested his forehead against hers.

"I need you now, Raina."

Smiling at his need, she wrapped her legs around his hips, as he had imagined earlier. Brushing her wetness against his hard cock caused the last of his resistance to fade away.

He glided inside her in one thrust, pushing past her barrier of resistance. She tensed in his arms at his intrusion. He realized at the last moment to take it easy on her. He never realized she would be a virgin. He expected her to be experienced with the life she lived. Charles called himself every sort a fool as he tried to pull out of her. But she only locked her legs tighter around him.

Bending over, he placed gentle kisses on her lips and whispered how sorry he was for hurting her. When he felt her body relax against his, he was brave enough to stare into her eyes. When he saw the midnight blue of her eyes darken with the same hunger he felt, he knew of her desire.

He pressed himself in deeper, and she tightened around his cock. Closing his eyes, he pressed deeper only to have her clench tighter. She held onto him as he slid deep inside her.

Raina saw him pause and realized he was holding himself back from hurting her more. Only he never hurt her. He took her by surprise, but none of it was pain. To finally have him inside her completed her. She needed to encourage his ravishment of her, and she knew the best way to do that was to show him of her pleasure.

Sliding her hands along his back, she slid them farther down over his buttocks. She squeezed them at the same time as she pressed her hips forward. She brought him hard into her core. She repeated this again. Looking into his eyes, she saw his struggle not to hurt her, but she was no fragile miss. She wanted him to unleash his passion on her. She wanted him to take her with all they both desired.

Smiling, she licked her tongue across her lips. Biting her bottom lip, she brought her hips up to him and slowly rotated her hips against his. She licked and tasted the salt on his neck as she kissed over to his ear.

"Take me Charles. I'm all yours," she whispered in his ear, then gently tugged his earlobe in between her teeth.

Charles growled and slid out of her, then back in swiftly. He repeated this over and over, his passion building. He could feel himself unraveling inside her. Their bodies were pressed tight together as he made love to her. She matched his rhythm thrust for thrust, both giving themselves to each other.

Raina let out a scream as she tightened around his cock, her wetness sliding between their legs. He thrust into her harder, wanting more, knowing she had not yet finished. Her fingers dug into his back as they reached higher in their climax. He sensed the moment she reached her fulfillment when she sobbed his name in pleasure over and over. With one final thrust into her, he reached his pleasure, her body wrapped tight around his.

Keeping her embraced in his arms, he rolled to the side. Not wanting to leave her body, he kept her close to him. As he felt their hearts beat against each other, he closed his eyes to the steady rhythm. The last he remembered before he drifted off to sleep was listening to her whisper his name over and over as she kissed his chest.

Chapter Twelve

UNTANGLING HERSELF FROM CHARLES'S arms, Raina slid herself off the bed. As she looked over her shoulder, she watched as Charles slept on. She slid on his discarded shirt. It brushed across her mid-thighs. As she buttoned the shirt, she walked over to gaze out the window.

Raina pulled the lace curtain aside and saw nothing but lush green hills surrounding them. She realized they were not at an inn after all. Charles had told her the truth. It looked like a private home. There was a lovely garden below her room filled with flowers and food. Raina took notice of how quiet it was, not only outdoors but inside as well.

Curious of their whereabouts, Raina opened the door to explore. Her bare feet wandered over the cold hardwood floors as she made her way along the hallways. She stopped to peek inside the rooms, looking for any other visitors. Every bedroom looked empty, except for being filled with familiar knickknacks to the owner of the room.

Raina made her way downstairs to continue her search. She found the library and parlor filled with comfortable but worn furniture. Obviously, this place didn't host guests, but was used for family only. She saw small miniatures of young children on the side tables. Picking one up, the frame showed two young children dressed in their Sunday best, frolicking on the ground with a puppy. She could see the joy and the love they shared. They were adorable children with blond hair and green eyes. Brother and sister. Charles and Ivy. Raina touched the photo, her fingers lingering over the boy. A sadness overcame her in that moment. The loss of her own brother at this age entered her mind. It was never far from her thoughts, as it was what fueled her revenge. But seeing this photo brought back her memories of happier times with her own brother.

With shaking fingers, she sat on the settee, holding the picture in her hands. Her thoughts were a jumble between imagining how Charles acted as a child to how her brother would have been now if he had the chance to live.

Startled by footsteps coming into the room, Raina set the picture on the table. An older woman came bustling in, carrying a tray filled with tea and sandwiches. Raina, embarrassed at her state of undress, tried pulling the shirt past her knees. When that failed, she grabbed at a pillow to cover herself.

"I thought I heard somebody in here. You must be famished, my dear," the old lady said as she set the tray on the table in front of Raina.

Raina sat in silence as the servant rattled on about insensitive men driving women through the night.

Mrs. Hobbs saw how unsure the young lady was in her discomfort and tried not to draw attention to the obvious. She could also tell how nervous she was. As soon as she had a private moment with the young man, she would give him a lecture on his list of priorities.

"I am Mrs. Hobbs, dear. Me and the mister are the caretakers of this cottage. If you are ever in need of something, you let one of us know. I take it young Mallory is still abed. He always was one to laze around in the mornings. What is your name, dearie?"

"I am—" Raina stopped herself. She almost told Mrs. Hobbs her true name. Running through the possibilities in her head of how safe it would be, she tried to think of an alias to tell the nice servant. As in all avenues of her life, the fewer individuals who realized her real identity the better. Raina could never forgive herself if something would happen to this innocent old lady because she knew her as Raina LeClair.

Before she told her one of her aliases, Charles sauntered into the room, wearing nothing but his breeches. His devilish smile shone at the predicament she had gotten herself into from wandering from the privacy of the bedroom. He had no decency in flaunting his body in front of the servant.

"Lady Raina Mallory is her name, my dear Mrs. Hobbs," Charles answered with a kiss upon the servant's cheek.

Raina became very still at this announcement. How dare he? Her anger began to boil underneath her calm façade. One of the many tricks her father taught her was to never let anyone see your anger, that way they would not recognize when your fury would strike.

"Oh, you have finally settled down. First Ivy, now you. And this must be your honeymoon. Now I understand the rush to get the cottage ready. Here I am thinking the worst of you. Congratulations, my dear boy, I must get started on a grand dinner for you, then Mr. Hobbs and I will make ourselves scarce for a couple of days," Mrs. Hobbs gushed on as she left the parlor.

Charles laughed at Mrs. Hobbs's excitement. He snatched a sandwich from the tray and ate it while waiting for her reaction.

"Will you pour the tea, Lady Mallory? Please eat a few sandwiches too. I would hate for you to waste away on our honeymoon."

Raina calmly poured his tea. She knew he waited for her to explode, but she did not show him her rage. Laying a couple of sandwiches on her plate, she sat back with ladylike precision and ate her small respite. Setting the plate on the table, she finished her tea. Patting her lips with a napkin, she sat back and folded her hands in her lap and waited.

Charles sat in a chair across from her and waited while she ate the sandwiches and drank her tea like a meek wife would appear. But he knew different. Just as Raina was not his wife, she was not a meek lady. She was fire and ice combined in one. Raina's icy demeanor impressed him. She was cool, composed, and under control. But he knew she was waiting to explode on him. He had a taste of her fire earlier and noticed it brimmed underneath the surface at this very moment.

Deciding that he wanted the fire to explode and burn out of control, he rose and closed the doors to the parlor. He locked the door and slid the key into the pocket of his breeches. Sitting on the settee next to her, he angled his body so that his chest pressed against her shoulder.

Bending his head, he whispered in her ear, "Shall we continue with our honeymoon, dearest?" he baited her.

Raina understood what he was doing. He wanted her to explode in anger at his audacity. He wanted her to confide in him and explain her plans for revenge. As much as he portrayed the lover upstairs, he was still the spy who put his country before everything—and everyone—else. She was not ready yet to put her trust in him. She may have given her body over to him earlier, but he did not have her heart. How would he respond if she turned the tables on him instead?

His warm breath caressed her neck, sending a warmth spreading over her body. She was aware of him as soon as he entered the room and flashed his smile at her. But it did not compare to the feelings she was having with him pressed against her side. Her body was hot and alive, aching for his touch again.

She felt her nipples harden against his shirt, the rough fabric scraping them. With the heat pooling between her legs, she shifted on the couch at her need for him. Raina closed her eyes and breathed in deeply, hoping to ease the ache for him again already.

He sensed what Raina was suffering, and Charles smiled at her discomfort. He saw her nipples harden underneath his shirt. Ah, the sight of her in it was making him hard for her. He wanted to unbutton his very own shirt and peel it from her body. When she shifted on the settee, he knew why and smiled, realizing her need as he pressed a kiss to the back of her ear.

Wanting her to discuss her feelings with him, he kept the pressure of their attraction building to new heights. Knowing she would pull away at any moment, he baited her again.

"I locked the door, so we can continue on this settee." Charles patted his hand on the cushion next to him.

Turning her head, she brushed her lips across his. At his stillness, she traced his lips with her tongue. When he still did not move, she gracefully slid across his lap, sliding her legs on both sides of his body and rising to her knees. Her fingers trailed through his hair, sinking into the soft thickness. Rounding the back of his neck, her fingertips came around to the front and slid across his chest. They traced lightly up and down.

As she bent over, her lips traced across his ear, slowly drawing his earlobe between her lips. Gently she sucked, feeling his hardness grow and press into her. Raina smiled as she whispered in his ear, "I thought we were continuing?"

Charles was as still as Michelangelo himself. He didn't dare move while she straddled his lap. It was heaven and hell combined. While he wanted nothing more to do than rip his shirt off her body, he needed answers. But heaven was overruling his thought process and would most definitely win. The temptation she was providing him was a reward for months of agony in trying to find her.

He made a promise to himself, this moment, this time. Then he would get the answers he wanted from her. But for now, he needed her. And she needed him. He sensed their need for each other from her touch to his body. Each stroke of her fingers set him aflame.

When he slid one hand up his shirt, he caressed her need. She was already wet and ready for him. With his other hand he pulled her head back and sank his lips on her throat. He took a deep breath and inhaled her passion, heat radiating off her neck.

His finger slid deep inside her, finding a rhythm which made her cry out. She gripped his shoulders as he stroked her. His mouth found its way to her lips, where he drank in her sweetness and desire. Her body was shaking in his arms, slowly unraveling bit by bit.

Raina knew she was playing a game with her taunt, but she no longer cared at the outcome. She needed him the same way she needed to breathe. She realized what could happen when she whispered those words.

Their kiss ignited their passions higher. Charles ripped the buttons off his shirt. They flew and scattered all over the parlor floor. The tiny buttons pinged across the hardwood floor like dice rolling across the table.

When he tugged his shirt down, he trapped her arms at her side. Her breasts spilled out for his delight. Urging her to her knees, he brought his head in between her breasts, his tongue tracing the valley that dipped between them. He followed the different paths they traveled. His hands moved to cup her breasts and brought them to his mouth to enjoy.

She was delicious.

One path led to her tight nipple, begging to be kissed. His tongue traced the red tip. As she wiggled on his lap, one of his hands clamped on her buttocks to hold her still. As he tilted his head to the side, he looked up. The look in her eyes was begging for him to kiss her. He took her nipple into his mouth and gently sucked. Charles watched as she closed her eyes and moaned.

He sucked her nipple harder and watched as her eyes opened in surprise. Moaning louder, she pressed her wetness into his chest. He experienced the slickness as she moved against him. He trailed his lips across to the other breast to please her there too.

As he sucked on her tight nipple, he had to touch her. Sliding his fingers into her core, they sunk into the honey sweetness. Her wetness dripped between his fingers at the onslaught of his passion toward her.

He needed to be in her now. His cock ached to slide deep into her center. Reaching up, he ripped his shirt off over her head and undid the placket of his pants. His cock sprang forward, brushing across her wetness.

Charles gripped her by her hips as he guided her onto his hardness. He moaned as her wetness surrounded him as she sank down around his cock. When she had settled as far as she could sink, he held her still on his lap, his fingers digging into her hips as he kept their bodies from moving. If he moved now, he would come. She was tight and wet, gripping his cock like a glove.

Raina was surprised at this position, but she did not show her innocence. He thought she was an experienced spy in every act. She saw his shock this morning when he realized she was a virgin, but he never spoke a word.

She yearned to be an experienced lady for him at that moment, but she had no clue on how to proceed. He was holding her still, and when she looked at him to question him with her eyes, she noticed his were closed. He was breathing deeply, and it seemed like he was trying to keep himself under control.

Raina hoped he wasn't done. Her body felt so alive with him inside her. She moved her hips slightly, and his fingers dug into her hips more. Ah, that felt so good. She tried it again, but this time she moved them more in a circle. Hearing a deep moan vibrate up his chest, Raina realized her power. As she kept moving her hips, she realized she was the one who had to set the tempo of this pleasure.

Her fingers sank into his shoulders as she found her grip. She moved her body up and down, her wetness gliding against his hardness. Charles threw his head back against the cushions as his hands helped guide her rhythm on his cock. She was a natural.

Her breasts teased against his chest, her tight nipples brushing across as she rose up and down. Raina's body moved faster as her body began to reach climax. He sensed her need as she tightened around his cock.

"Charles," she moaned.

He could hear the need in her voice as her body tightened in his arms. Pulling her close, he moved his hips with her. He gripped her buttocks as he slid deep inside her. Holding her still, he rotated his hips into hers. He felt her wetness clinging to him and knew she was ready to explode.

"Kiss me, Raina," he demanded.

Her lips kissed him hungrily. Over and over they laid claim to her need to taste him. That was all it took for him to drive himself into her. He slid in deeply then pulled out and repeated himself. Her kisses became more erratic, her need spilling forth as she devoured his lips. He slid out and waited. Her lips stilled against his.

Waiting. Wanting. Needing.

He slid inside her so slowly that he felt every moment as her body exploded around him. Her kisses turning slow and sweet as she melted into his arms. When he entered her fully and completely with her desire enveloping him in sweetness, he came alive in her.

Chapter Thirteen

CHARLES PULLED RAINA IN close to his body and held her, softly running his fingers through her dark hair trailing down her back. They lay there wrapped in each other's arms, content in the moment. Neither one of them wanted to break the spell. They kept to their own thoughts, afraid words would break the fragile bond they shared moments before.

Raina closed her eyes as Charles moved out from underneath her. He gently lay her on the settee. She opened her eyes as she felt a light blanket covering her body. Charles knelt in front of her, brushing her hair back out of her eyes.

"I will have Hobbs run a bath for you, and then we will enjoy the wonderful dinner Mrs. Hobbs is making for us. After that, we must talk."

Raina nodded her head to him. She was too choked with emotion from the passion they shared to argue with him. Especially since she knew he was correct.

Charles rose to answer the knock on the door. She stared as he slid his trousers up his long muscular legs. As he buttoned up the placket, Raina saw the evidence of his desire. Looking up in question, she caught his eyes as he watched her looking at him.

Smiling, he winked at her. "Yes, my love," he answered her unasked question.

Raina blushed and looked away. She heard him laughing from the doorway. He was impossible.

Charles laughed at her innocence. He thought nothing would make Raina LeClair blush, but obviously his desire for her caught her unaware. Oh, he would have great pleasure in showing her all the delights they were going to share.

Charles opened the door a crack and directed Hobbs to ready a bath for Raina. He lowered his voice and directed Hobbs on other matters to arrange. They needed to prepare for any obstacle that would come their way in the next couple of weeks. While only family had knowledge of the cottage, they still remained in danger, because if anyone wanted someone located, they could make it happen with the right information and money.

Walking back to her, he held out his hand. As she slid her hand into his, their fingers entwined. It was then he knew he had gained her trust. He wrapped the blanket around her delectable body. Her hair was a tangled mess hanging around her shoulders, mussed to the right degree. Her lips were full and pouty from their kisses, begging for him to kiss them again. But it was her eyes that captured his attention. He noticed the weariness leaving them, replaced with hope. Hope that he needed to bloom. Bloom into the love he wanted to share with her.

He lifted her into his arms and carried her from the parlor and into the bedroom. Pulling the blanket from her body, he gently lowered her into the steamy tub. The steam floated through the air as the scent of roses filled their senses. The water was sprinkled with rose petals.

Charles lowered himself into the water with her, pulling her back into his arms. Lifting a petal, he traced it over her body. He stared at the silky-smooth petal gliding over her figure. Her body was as smooth as the petal. When he guided the petal over her nipples, he looked as they tightened into soft buds, begging for more. His fingers drifted across them with the water lightly brushing them. He felt her relax back into him, sighing softly.

Lifting a bar of rose-scented soap off the chair next to the tub, he washed her body. He slid the soap across her curves, molding the soap to his hands at his attentions. She was so soft and supple and fit his body to perfection.

Raina closed her eyes at his gentle care. While his hardness pressed into her back, she knew this was not about giving in to his desires. He was taking care of her. The way he held her and washed her showed her his feelings for her.

The touch of his hands were protective and loving. Raina let herself relax against him. It had been so long since anybody had cared for her. She savored the feelings so she would remember them after she left him. She would remember this memory more than all the others. It was the moment she finally realized the depth of what he felt for her, and it was too much for her. But she was selfish and wanted more, so she lay there and soaked in the time they had together.

Charles spoke to her quietly, so as not to frighten her.

"When I awoke after we made love this morning and you were gone, I was frightened you had vanished again."

Raina listened as he talked in his soft, soothing voice. He spoke so gently, as if he was talking to a wounded animal.

"It seemed to be every time you were within my grasp you would disappear. I have searched for you for months. Every emotion a man can feel toward a woman, I have felt toward you. I almost convinced myself you were not worth the trouble. But every night when I would close my eyes I'd picture the tortured look in yours and remember the care you gave me. The care and love that saved my life. I owe you my life."

"You owe me nothing, Charles."

"That is where you are wrong, my dear. I owe you the same gift you gave to me."

Raina rolled over, water splashing onto the floor. She pressed the front of her wet, slick body into his. She trailed her fingers over the droplets of water on his chest.

"But I have given you no gifts."

"You gave me the gift in believing. Believing when, no matter the depth of somebody's deception, there is innocence lurking beneath. With innocence, there is a heart portraying what is true in the end."

"Those are a fool's thoughts."

"Then I am a fool."

Raina rolled back over and sat up. She stood, reaching for the towel, and dried off her body. She felt too vulnerable lying in the tub with him. Not only was her body naked, but also her soul. She recognized in his eyes what was reflecting in hers. He thought to save her. But she did not want his salvation or his gratitude. What she desired from him was too huge a wish to think she could have.

Wandering over to her valise, she pulled out a dress for dinner. She would play along with his little marital scene for the servants' sake. She would even discuss the information Charles sought, but that was where it ended. There would be no happily ever after where the hero saves the heroine from all that is evil. Raina grasped of no other way of life than the one she had. She witnessed enough destruction throughout her lifetime to know better. Those were the fantasies of fairy tales or the stories in romance novels. Not the ever after of a spy whose main goal was to destroy the exact people who ruined her life.

Charles finished his bath watching her dress. He regarded her quiet, pensive mood and saw the gears working in her mind. She might be resigned to her circumstances for the time being, but he knew she was already planning her escape route. He would let her plan, but he would not let her follow through with any of them.

Stepping from the tub, he dried off, wrapping the towel around his hips as he went to her. She had her back to him as she looked out the window. He did the buttons up her dark green gown. It was not elegant by any means, but serviceable for her needs, he imagined. The need for her to slip in and out without being noticed. The only downfall to her plans was that by herself, dressed in rags would draw attention to her, which was probably why she always wore such hideous makeup to disguise her true beauty.

There was no other beauty compared to her in his eyes. From her long, dark hair tumbled in waves around her shoulders to the curves wrapped around her body, she was every man's fantasy. But to him, it was her eyes that drew him to her. They held a vulnerability only he could see, which was how he could read her. He knew when she was scheming, sad, and when her desire for him was strong. But there was one feeling he never witnessed—happiness. It was an emotion he wanted to see reflected in her dark eyes. He wanted to see them lighten with joy.

"We are at my parents' cottage. They used to come here to escape the pressures of society."

"Where is here?" Raina asked, trying to find out her exact whereabouts.

Charles ignored her question.

"They brought me here when I was young. It has gotten little use in the last few years."

"Why?"

"It was hard for my father to come back here. The place holds too many memories of my mother."

"What happened to your mother?"

"She died from a fever a few years after Ivy was born. She contacted pneumonia after getting caught in a rainstorm," Charles explained.

"I am sorry for your loss," Raina murmured.

Charles pulled her back into his arms and pressed a kiss to the back of her head. He held her there as they watched the sun set across the open fields. The fiery gaze stretched out for miles as it began its descent into sleep. It turned to a pale orange as it tried to stay awake, granting the open country a few more moments of light.

Charles turned Raina around and kissed her playfully on the nose.

"Shall we do justice to Mrs. Hobbs's dinner, my dear Lady Mallory," he teased, wanting to see her smile.

Raina granted him a small grin. As she looked him up and down, she arched her eyebrow at him and whispered in her husky French accent, "You are a bit underdressed for our wedding feast, Lord Mallory."

Charles threw back his head and laughed. His laughter vibrated off them in waves, encouraging her to relax with him. She joined in his laughter with her own small chuckle. As he pulled away from her to dress, Raina was chilled at the loss of his embrace. When he threw her a smile over his shoulder, she felt his heat warm her again. His enjoyment filled her with a sense of belonging, of something more powerful than she could imagine. It was the joy of contentment, of belonging again to someone more than herself.

After Charles had finished dressing in a fresh shirt and trousers, he offered his arm to her. She noted he had dressed plain to make her feel more comfortable. No cravats, vest, or suit coat. He did not need to portray the aristocratic gentleman. He was only a man escorting his "wife" to dinner in their country cottage.

As they made their way to the small dining room situated in the back corner of the cottage, they breathed the delicious aromas of Mrs. Hobbs's dinner. She had set up the table in a romantic setting, with candles in the center. Next to Raina's plate lay a single red rose. The rest of the tabletop's dishes were filled with so many delicacies. Raina could see smoked duck, roasted asparagus, and tiny potatoes in a creamy sauce, but it was what sat in the center that brought tears to her eyes. There next to the candles sat a small wedding cake. It was decorated with tiny pink roses made from icing. Raina could tell Mrs. Hobbs made the cake with love.

She felt guilty for deceiving the kind woman. Since there was not a thing she could do about it, she decided to enjoy her time with Charles. When it came time for her to leave, she would apologize for their deception.

Charles sat her in her chair, and Raina picked up the rose to smell. Lowering her head, she brought the flower to her nose, smelling in the sweet fragrance while covering her eyes. She did not want Charles to realize the effect the table had on her.

Charles sat next to her, pulling his chair up to the small table. Mrs. Hobbs had outdone herself once again. He needed to reward her handsomely for this. It was perfect. He watched the effect it had on Raina and knew his plan was working. Now all Charles wanted was for the evening to work its magic. To let things progress slowly would be the only way to capture her heart.

Over the course of dinner, Charles was the ultimate gentleman. He did not pressure Raina into discussing her "adventures." Instead, he regaled her with stories of his youth, making her laugh at the jokes he would pull on Ivy and his grand exploits with his friends. His charming attitude even relaxed Raina into sharing a few of her fond memories of her brother. It was the first time since his death that the pain of losing him wasn't so intense. Maybe it was the way Charles listened to her and asked questions that drew her out of the shell of pain she surrounded herself with. It was as if a giant weight was lifting from her heart. Instead of only remembering pain, she could now remember the joy he had brought to her life.

There would never be a day that went by that she wouldn't miss her parents and brother. The pain and loneliness were too deep to ever forget, but talking with Charles made her recall the fond memories and the love she felt for them. That was what she needed to remember and feel the most.

Charles could see Raina unwinding as they discussed their youth. He saw the weariness leave her eyes. While they still showed deep sadness, exhaustion, and a small amount of fear, he also saw a spark of life. A spark he wanted to enlarge to a flame.

Raina eyed the scrumptious cake sitting before them.

"It looks too lovely to eat," Raina sighed.

Charles laughed. "But we must, dear wife. We do not want to hurt Mrs. Hobbs's feelings, do we?"

Raina joined in with his laughter. "Of course not, dear husband. We must do her cake the justice it deserves."

Raina pulled the cake toward them. She handed Charles a fork. With a wink at him, she dug her fork into the delicious cake. The moist cake slid between her lips, dissolving in her mouth. Bringing the fork slowly out of her mouth, she made sure to lick off every drop of sweet frosting along the way. She moaned in delight as she licked her lips.

"Oh, that was amazing. You must try a bite, Lord Mallory."

Charles groaned inwardly at the sight of Raina eating cake. He would never have thought the mere sight of a woman taking a bite of cake could fuel his desires. The image she portrayed as she licked her fork clean turned him hard as stone. He wanted to be the frosting she licked off her lips. He imagined doing more than that with the frosting.

"Don't mind if I do, Lady Mallory," he said as he dipped his finger into the frosting on the cake and brought it to his lips. He slid his finger into his mouth, sampling the sweet confection.

Raina's eyes grew large, and she gulped as she watched him savor the frosting. How did he make a mere bite looks so sensual? She stared as he dipped his finger through the frosting again, only this time he coated her lips with it. She guided her tongue around her lips, savoring the sweet taste.

Charles leaned over and joined his tongue with hers, nibbling on her lips. Kissing her slowly, he drew out every sweet flavor between their lips. Their tongues tangled into long, slow strokes that filled their souls. The kiss controlled their senses, where the only thing they felt or tasted was one another. Their needs poured over into the all-consuming kiss that soon became soul shattering.

Charles pulled back from the kiss and gently pressed one more upon her lips.

"Mmm, yes. Amazing."

Then he pulled back and ate the cake as if the kiss had not even transpired between them. He caught her watching him in a daze and winked at her. He nodded toward the cake for her to join him.

Raina couldn't believe how he sat there eating the darn cake so nonchalantly, as if they had not shared the most powerful kiss she'd ever had in her life. Then he did the unexpected and reached for her hand. She noticed the small tremble and the pressure of his control. Looking up into his eyes, she saw his desire but realized he was holding himself back. It was then Raina understood. He was giving her time. Time she needed to heal. He would be there for her in every way that mattered.

Raina smiled up at him then—a smile of gratitude. She picked up her fork and joined him in eating the most delicious cake she had ever tasted.

Chapter Fourteen

MAKING HER WAY ALONG the garden path, Raina took in the magnificent colors surrounding her. The flowers were awakening from a deep sleep this morning. Drops of dew glistened on their petals, some dropping like pearls into the air. As she took a deep breath, Raina drew in the sweet air of the country. Relaxing for the first time in months, she let her fingers glide across the top of the flowers. Coming to a rose bush, she noticed a few petals had fallen from a rose. She bent over and picked up the discarded petals. Carrying them in her palm, she sat upon the bench nearby.

She spread them in her lap, her fingers going over the soft, smooth texture. They formed around her fingers. Bringing one to her face, she caressed the petal across her cheek, smiling to herself of the simple pleasure, and closed her eyes. Raina sat there for a while and let the sun warm her spirits.

Lost in her thoughts, she was unaware that Charles had joined her on the bench. She knew he wanted to talk. Last night after dinner, he'd escorted her to her own room. After placing a chaste kiss upon her lips, he wished her sweet dreams. She lay in bed wondering at his act of chivalry when she drifted off to sleep.

"What dangerous game are you playing?" he asked her.

"I am not playing any games, Mallory. I am only out for revenge."

"Look where revenge landed you last time."

She turned her head toward him and gave him a bittersweet smile. "I would have never met you if it wasn't for that revenge."

"But you were ultimately wrong in your vengeance."

"Yes, but I am correct this time. This time I will destroy the man who destroyed my family."

"It will destroy you in the end. It has already begun to."

"I don't see any other way. He must be stopped."

"And I will stop him, but not at the expense of losing you."

"But you do not have me."

"Don't I?" Charles asked as he fingered the lace around her shoulders. He rubbed the fabric between his fingers.

Raina moved her shoulders out of his reach.

"Just because you bedded me twice does not mean you own me, Mallory."

Charles leaned closer to her, sliding his hand around to her neck. He rubbed her tension away, showing her a patience that made her weary. His thumb worked into her skin, easing her tight muscles into jelly. He bent his head to whisper in her ear, "I never said I owned you."

Raina rose from the bench and moved a few paces away. She could not think with him touching her and whispering in her ear. He took over her emotions to where all she did was feel. And she had no room for feelings in this time and place. Looking over, she saw him sprawled out, his arms spread wide across the back of the bench. He had one leg thrown over the other, crossed over his knee. As calm and carefree as he tried to portray, Raina saw the one thing that gave him away. He couldn't keep his foot still. His shoe bounced up and down through the air. Not fast and quick, but enough for Raina to see his agitation.

Her father had trained her to take notice of the people surrounding her. Everybody always displayed body language that gave away their true feelings. So, while it would appear Charles was waiting to be patient, his foot showed that wanted answers sooner than later.

"Why did you go to Blackstone's?"

"Your sister needed me to deliver a letter of apology."

"You knew he was involved with Shears. How could you put yourself in that danger?"

"But you are forgetting, I wasn't at risk. I was Ivy Thornhill's companion, Mrs. Whitlow, who was delivering a personal message to his lordship," Raina said in her Mrs. Whitlow impersonation.

Charles glared at her sarcasm.

"Exactly how personal did the message end up being, Raina?"

"I did not kill him, Charles. He was already stabbed when his butler showed me into his study."

"Then why didn't his butler help him?"

"He was unaware of his injury. When the butler closed the door, his lordship motioned for me to come closer. He grabbed my arm and whispered that I was next, laughing as he died. What I do not comprehend is how he realized who I was."

"This is where you are naïve in the game we play. Every player in this game knows their opponents and what their next moves will be. That is why we continue going around in circles until one of us can outsmart our enemy. This game will continue for years. I, for one, am ready for this to end. The lives of too many of my loved ones are at stake."

Raina paced back and forth along the path in the garden, listening to him. She still didn't understand how her identity was leaked. She had been so careful in her disguises, and she had fooled many people, including the Thornhills. There was only one man she trusted with her secrets, and he would not betray her, would he? If so, he was also betraying Mallory and the Thornhills. Was he friend or foe?

"Maxwell."

"What about him?"

"He was the only one who had knowledge of my whereabouts, and wasn't he the one who was present when you were beaten again?"

Charles shook his head in denial.

"It was not him. I recognize he is in a bad place and cannot be trusted, but Maxwell would not intentionally put either one of us in danger."

"He will if it will gain him the information he desires more than everything else."

"He is on our side. He is undercover.

"Maxwell is after his own agenda, don't you see? He is not working to stop Shears. He is after information only Shears holds. Maxwell is nothing but Shears's pawn. Maxwell will help destroy us if he can gain what he most desires."

"And what is that, my dear?

"You are supposedly his trusted friend. Don't you know?"

He didn't want to believe Maxwell could betray him to Shears. Maybe he was in trouble and ought to be extracted. No, she was wrong. Maxwell was playing his cover well if he was able to fool everybody that trusted in him. He needed to convince Raina that Maxwell was on their side.

"Maxwell will not betray his friends and country for any reason. He is but playing a part in this game. He must gain Shears's trust to help end him. If along the way he must pass him information, he would not give him any details that would put us in harm's way."

Raina could see she was not getting through to Charles. She kneeled between his knees and grabbed hold of his hands.

"I realize this is hard for you to believe, but for everybody's sake, you need to see your once trusted friend has gone over to the enemy's side. For whatever reason, he is no longer one of you, and he cannot be trusted."

Charles acknowledged the unspoken truth of her words. There were signs of Maxwell's betrayal—Charles's own kidnapping last year to be precise. In the end, Maxwell had come clean and made his rescue possible. In the last few months, he did not want to admit this to himself, let alone anybody else, but his suspicions grew on which side his partner was fighting for.

"On the night of Blackstone's death, where were you disappearing to?" Charles changed the subject on her.

Raina sighed and pushed herself up and away from him. As she edged farther away, she guessed they had finished discussing Maxwell, and he wanted to move on to her. She walked away to a path she spied earlier. The trail led her into a wooded area. The trees wrapped around the path, their roots coming out of the ground. She pressed her hands against the rough bark as she used them to guide herself along the path.

She heard him follow her. He did not try to help her along the path but waited patiently while she picked her way along the trail. After a while, she saw sunshine beating an opening to the path she took. Walking toward it, she wandered into an open field filled with bluebells. Their purple petals swayed in the open breeze. Raina stopped and breathed in their earthly scent. It was a vision to behold. The field stretched for miles, filled with nothing but wildflowers. She turned around in a circle with her arms spread wide, closing her eyes she let the peace and tranquility soak into her soul.

Charles watched as the peaceful setting wrapped itself around Raina. As she twirled around in circles, he saw the magic of the place seep into her being. When she took off at a run, he did not chase after her. He waited for her. Charles would wait for her forever. He saw that his questions scared her, made her open and vulnerable to him, which was something she was not used to being. So, he could wait until she was ready.

Raina ran across the open field. She knew there was no escape. It was obvious they were deep in the countryside. She was not running away from him. When she had stepped out of the wooden path and into the open air, she noticed a weight had been lifted from her soul. The pressure of her mission was slipping out of her grasp. Everything that was important before seemed meaningless now. By no means was the loss of her family meaningless, but the vengeance for them was. After she avenged them, what then? It would not bring them back to her.

She sank to the damp ground, her skirts billowing around her legs. Tears cascaded down her cheeks, running in rivulets to drop upon the bluebells. Wiping the moisture off her cheeks, she had not realized she had been crying. She gasped as the pain of loss hit her. Her eyes filled and ran over with an outpouring of fresh tears as she cried at the loss she had suffered. The pain appeared so open and raw, as if it had only happened recently. They had been dead for years, but she had never grieved for them. Raina had only been out for revenge.

Where had revenge gotten her? Wanted for a murder, she did not commit. It finally dawned on her that very revenge could get her hanged for treason. For a long time, she did not care because it could reunite her with her family again. But now everything had changed. She wanted to live. She wanted to enjoy the open breeze on her skin. She wanted to walk in her bare feet across fields of wildflowers. Raina wished to feel the touch and kiss of a man. She wanted his love.

When the last of her tears settled on the gentle curve of the bluebells, Raina stared as the sunlight kissed them away. She looked around and noticed Charles had not followed her. He trusted her not to leave. If he trusted her, maybe in time he could love her too.

Raina slid her slippers off her feet and rose to make her way back to Charles. Her feet sank into the softness of the flowers. Petals slid between her toes, tickling the soles of her feet. She smiled at the simplicity of life.

Charles had lay back on the grass, his arms behind his head. His eyes were closed, but he knew she stood over him. Keeping his eyes closed, he waited for her to speak. He knew she would return to him. He wanted to run after her and help her with her pain but recognized she needed the time to herself. He knew you couldn't heal those around you. You could only show them you were near when they needed you. Everybody must grieve in their own way.

Laying on the grass next to him, she let the sunlight wrap itself around her, warming her from the outside in.

"My mother used to do that. Run through the flowers in her bare feet. She would tell me the fairies tickled her feet as she ran. I brought Ivy here when she was young and told her stories of our mother."

"Your mother sounds like she was carefree."

"She was wild as the wind, my father always says."

"How so?"

"She always acted first, then would think second. She was a passionate lady who wanted to enjoy life. London always stifled her. They had to spend time there when Parliament was in session, as Father was very involved in politics. But whenever there was a break, he would whisk us here to get away. When we visited the cottage, they could be themselves. It was here where she caught her illness."

Raina reached between them and laced their fingers together. Squeezing gently, she urged him to continue his story.

"It was raining gently; the sun was shining, but it was still raining. Mother, in her impulsiveness of life, ran out in the rain, dancing through the garden. Father urged her to come inside, but Mother only laughed and encouraged him to join her. I remember him gathering her cloak and wrapping her inside it. They shared a kiss, which was nothing new for us to see. They were always affectionate in front of us. I smiled at their silliness. Then the kiss turned different, and Mrs. Hobbs shuffled me away with promises of sugar cookies in the kitchen."

Charles reflected to himself on what the kiss had changed into. It was from one of love to passion—the kind he now felt toward Raina. Charles finally understood the loss his father experienced. He felt the same feelings for Raina that his father felt for his mother. He grasped how the loss of his mother had affected his father with a deep sadness he could never comprehend until now.

"The next day, my mother became ill. The storms had become so heavy in the area, and they washed out the bridges. Father was not able to get a doctor for her. Mrs. Hobbs and my father did everything they could for her, but they could not save her. My father has been consumed in his grief for years. I know now how losing somebody can make you do crazy things, but in the end, they are still gone. You need to remember the times you spent with them and treasure those moments close to your heart."

Raina turned her body toward Charles, lying on her side. Her head was cradled in the crook of her arm.

"Where are we?" Raina asked.

"Near Dover."

"Aren't you afraid I will flee?"

Charles turned to face her. With his free hand, he lifted the strand of hair that had come loose from her braid and slid it behind her ear.

"No."

"How can you be so certain?"

"Because you are tired of running."

"It is all I am capable of doing."

"Then take this time and rest."

"When are we leaving?"

"When I can see it is safe to leave."

"After we leave, where will we go?"

"It depends."

"On what?"

"The outcome."

"The outcome from what?"

"The circumstances."

"What circumstances?" Raina asked in frustration. He was talking in riddles.

Charles laughed. He rolled back over and watched the clouds float across the sky. Raina growled at his silence. Rolling over, she threw her hand over her eyes, blocking out the sunshine. When she sensed a shadow hanging over her, she opened her eyes to see the rolling puffs of clouds blocking the sun.

"We would lie like this sometimes and imagine the clouds to be different items. He had an overactive imagination. They were always monsters of some sort," Raina whispered.

"Were you close?"

"Oh yes. There was a huge age gap, but when Mama had him, he was a joy. She had tried for years to give Papa a son. I guess that was why Papa trained me. He had given up hope of ever having a boy. When she finally did, he was spoiled by all of us."

"He made up stories of monsters and dragons and regaled us at dinner with his tall tales. We all doted on him. When his and Mama's carriage crashed, it devastated Papa. That was when he wanted out. He suspected their deaths weren't an accident. He thought Napoleon had them killed."

"Why would Napoleon have them killed? I thought your father was a high-ranking general in his army?"

"Mama was sick after having Matisse. Papa wanted to retire, but they would not let him. Once you join, you cannot leave. Something went horribly wrong with a deal involving Shears. Papa feared for their safety, so he sent Mama and Mattie away to a safe house, but along the way, the carriage crashed, killing them instantly."

"Why were you not with them?"

"I was away at school in England."

"Why did you attend school in England and not in France near your family?"

"Papa wanted me to work on my speech. He wanted me to have an English accent when I spoke."

"So that is how you are able to move around in disguise so easily. I have spent the last few months looking for a French woman because that is how you spoke when you took care of me."

"When I am not in disguise, my French becomes more pronounced if I choose it to be. At the time, I was conflicted in my role as a kidnapper and caretaker with you. I thought speaking in French would confuse you and aid me when I needed to leave."

"How was your father able to keep you safe?"

"Your friend Thornhill."

"I am confused. How does a French general and an English spy know each other."

"I told you my father wanted out. He knew of Thornhill and went to him, promising war secrets for new identities for me and him. He arranged to have me escorted from my school to his ship, where my father waited. Once I was on the ship, we sailed to a safe location. Only it wasn't. We were ambushed. My father instructed me to stay below when the ship was attacked. After I heard the fighting had stopped, I came on deck. My father was lying in a pool of blood. I reacted to the only thing I realized: my father was dead and the only individuals who knew of our existence on the ship were Thornhill and his men. So, I grabbed my knife and stabbed Thornhill. I thought if it was not for him, my father could be alive today."

"He was not at fault, Raina."

"But he was in a way, Charles."

"How so?"

"The man who escorted me from school to Thornhill's ship is the same one who introduced me to Shears. The same man who helped me to kidnap you last year."

"Maxwell?" Charles asked.

"The one same. That is why I told you he cannot be trusted. Knowing what I know now, he is the one responsible for the death of my father. He has been selling our secrets to Shears."

Charles lay in silence to her declarations. None of it made sense to the character of his friend. Thorn warned him of Maxwell's involvement with Shears, but Charles had chalked it up to Maxwell working undercover to bring down Shears down. Now more evidence pointed to Maxwell's deception. What did Shears have that Maxwell wanted?

Charles rose to his feet and held out his hands to Raina. Sliding her hands in his, he pulled her to her feet. He laced his fingers with hers and walked them back to the cottage. He never spoke to her, but let their silence guide him in his decision to investigate Maxwell's connection with Shears. Maybe there were more reasons to his deception than Charles wanted to believe. In the meantime, they would spend some isolated time at the cottage. Hopefully, Thornhill would find out what Charles needed to know before he moved forward on his destruction of Shears. He only hoped that in his plans for destruction he did not lose a friend or the woman he was falling in love with.

Chapter Fifteen

CHARLES WANDERED THROUGH THE cottage looking for Raina. He made his way to the kitchen, where she could usually be found helping Mrs. Hobbs. When he didn't find her there, he went outside to the gardens. While the garden showed signs of neglect over the years, it came to life over the past couple of weeks. She had pulled weeds and trimmed back the disarray of entangled vines. She even managed to convince him to help her. A couple of afternoons last week, they spent a few hours taming the garden into the peaceful oasis his mother always meant it to be. As he walked along the paths, he thought of his mother and her joy of working in these very gardens. He smiled at the gift Raina gave him. To be able to remember his mother in such a happy memory.

When he didn't locate her there, he wandered to the stables. He did not find her there either. Mr. Hobbs informed him he saw her wandering toward the cliffs with a book. Thinking of a surprise for her, he made his way back to the cottage. He talked Mrs. Hobbs into making them a basket for a picnic. She thought it was a wonderful idea, to surprise his wife with lunch. She filled the basket as she praised him on being such a romantic husband. Charles felt guilty for the lie, but not enough to risk Raina's life with the truth.

As he gathered a blanket and the picnic basket, Charles set out to find his lovely bride. He found her sitting under a large oak tree at the edge of the woods. A book lay open in her lap, her finger running along the edge of the pages. She wasn't reading the book, but lost in thought, staring out at the open field.

She had on a simple day dress in which Mrs. Hobbs had helped her hem. It was one of Ivy's old dresses. Her hair was pulled back in a simple braid, with a few pieces loose and blowing in the breeze. Charles stared as she closed her eyes and leaned her head back against the tree. Her body was relaxed as it enjoyed the fresh open air. Charles could not recall ever seeing her at such peace. His decision to stay at the cottage was proving to be the best idea he'd ever had.

Lost in watching her, he shifted and stepped on a tree branch. It snapped and broke the stillness of the moment. Raina glanced up swiftly at the disturbance to see him in the distance. He smiled sheepishly and started toward her.

Raina smiled shyly at him. She pulled the stray bits of her hair behind her ear. She rose to her feet and waited for him to join her near the tree.

"I come bearing gifts," he explained.

"What sort of gifts?"

"Lunch. I hope I am not disturbing you. I thought we could sit by the cliffs and watch the boats as we eat."

"No, I would love the company," she said as she reached for the blanket.

They walked closer to the cliffs for their luncheon. Raina spread out the blanket, lowering herself and adjusting her skirts around her legs. Charles knelt next to her, sitting the picnic basket between them.

"I enlisted Mrs. Hobbs to pack us a lunch. She thought it very romantic of me to surprise my wife," Charles teased.

Raina blushed as she unpacked the basket. She knew he was only teasing, but it was an awkward position they were in with their lies. Mrs. Hobbs apparently thought their marriage needed these romantic gestures, considering they were sleeping in separate bedrooms. Even though the kind housekeeper never asked, she noted the questions in her eyes. The first day they were at the cottage, their lovemaking was obvious to the declaration of their marriage. In the weeks that followed, the servant had to wonder at their lack of intimacy. She wasn't the only one who wondered. Raina was in constant woolgathering over the situation. Charles started off all hot, then turned cold. He was by no means indifferent to her, but he pulled back. There was still the soft brush of his hand against hers from time to time and his gazes toward her when he assumed she was not looking, which she always was. She could not get enough of him. Her eyes followed him whenever he was near. When he wasn't, she searched for him, wanting any sign from him that he wanted her too.

But she was only disappointed. She was so lonely for him even though he was close. She wanted to share their connection again, but every night it was the same. They retired to the parlor after dinner, where he would engage her in a game of chess or read a book to her. Then he escorted her to her room with a polite kiss to her hand, wishing her sweet dreams. She would then crawl between the covers and think of him holding her in his arms, whereupon she drifted off to her sweet dreams. Sweet dreams of him exploring her body with his touch and kisses. She would awaken each morning, restless with a need she could not explain. She would search for him for any attention he would give her. But today was different when she awoke. Raina was disappointed with herself for becoming vulnerable to him. While she ached for his attention, she knew she was becoming too dependent on Charles. When she decided to leave, it would hurt too much to part from him. Which was why she was spending the afternoon by herself. After she picked a book from the library shelf, she made her way to the open fields to daydream the day away. Her time here was ending. She wanted a day of no fear and only happy memories to last her through her final mission.

Charles watched as the blush stole over her cheeks. He wanted to place soft kisses along the curve of her neck where the blush disappeared too. Charles was frustrated from playing the gentleman to her these past few weeks. He thought he sensed her frustration too when she would seek him out every day. When she did not come looking for him today, Charles worried he had pushed her away. He thought he owed her space from rushing their relationship the first day they arrived. He'd hoping that with space she would welcome his advances. Playing the gentlemen had gotten him nowhere but empty nights in his bed chamber. The chaste kiss he gave her every night drove him to cool dips in the pond before he spent restless nights in his bed, wanting her with a desperate need. He hoped this picnic would play into his plans for seduction. Their time here was ending. He needed to convince her of his desire and his plans for their future.

"That was kindhearted of her. I am afraid I have been in her way this week."

"No, my dear, you have been great company for her. She misses having a woman around to chat with. It has been a while since Ivy has visited the cottage."

"Will Ivy still come to visit?" Raina inquired as she set out the contents of the basket.

"Yes, Thorn and Ivy will bring the children for a visit as soon as she can travel," Charles answered as he popped a grape into his mouth.

Raina slapped his hands away from the food as she continued unpacking the basket. It appeared Mrs. Hobbs had included the entire kitchen.

Charles laughed at her sternness. He pulled out a bottle of wine, uncorking it and pouring out two glasses for them to drink as Raina loaded two plates with cheese, meats, crackers, and fruit. Passing her a glass, they ate in silence, as they smiled at each other between bites.

Charles drew her out in conversation about everything and nothing in particular. He loved listening to her talk and loved discussing important matters with her. He kept the conversation light, with small jokes in between. She sat with her arms propping her body up, relaxed. She took small bites in between her discussion of the book she was reading. Charles regarded her animated face as she regaled him with bits of the comedy. It was refreshing to see her so happy. He wanted to make her smile and laugh this way every day.

She lay back, her hand covering her stomach.

"Oh, I am so full. Once again, Mrs. Hobbs has done justice to a terrific meal."

"Oh, but we are not finished yet, my dear."

Raina sat up and pulled the basket to her. As she looked inside, she saw a piece of their wedding cake nestled to the back corner.

"Well, it will hurt her feelings if we do not eat it," Raina commented as she pulled the cake from the basket.

"How right you are, my dear," Charles replied, handing her a fork.

Raina sank the fork into the dessert, the moist cake clinging to the prongs. Instead of sliding the delicious piece into her mouth, she brought the morsel to his lips. He opened his mouth as she guided the piece between them. As he closed his mouth over the cake, she gently brought the fork back as his lips wiped the frosting away. He licked his lips, watching for her reaction. She dipped the fork back into the cake and fed herself a bite. She repeated his action of licking her lips.

He leaned across from her, wiping his thumb across her lips. Pink frosting coated his thumb as he brought it to his mouth. Slowly sucking his thumb in, he licked off the frosting.

"Mmm. Delicious," Charles moaned.

Charles's tongue replaced his thumb. He gently licked the frosting away from her lips, dipping inside her mouth for a taste.

"Yes, most definitely delicious."

Charles pulled Raina into his arms and kissed her deeply. Soft, slow, deep kisses that seemed to last for hours but were only mere seconds. Lowering her body on the blanket, he pulled her tight against him. His hands roamed her body over her dress.

Raina moaned against his lips. Her body melted against his. She needed to touch him. As she glided her hand down, she pulled his shirt from his trousers. Her palms slid up, touching his chest. She felt as he sucked in his breath at her touch. Her fingers trailed up and down his chest, touching him with featherlight caresses. Her touch became bolder as her hand skimmed lower.

She could feel his hardness pressed against her stomach. He was so powerful. Becoming braver, her hand slid over the front of his trousers, brushing across him. His grip on her tightened as she rubbed her hand back and forth. Charles's kiss stopped as he hissed in a breath. His head fell backward as he breathed in a gulp of air. Raina gazed at him as he fought an inner struggle. When he tilted his head back toward her, she saw the fire of desire light up his eyes. Desire for her.

Her fingers slid over the buttons, slowly undoing them. She watched as his eyes darkened to a forest green that matched the woods behind them. Peeling the placket of his trousers back, she guided her hand inside. Raina slid her hand around his warmth and enfolded him in her palm. Wrapping her fingers around him, she stroked him, one long, slow stroke after another.

He pulled her head to him and ravished her lips. He drank from her lips every ounce of passion she had for him. His kisses became greedier as she stroked him in her slow seduction. The slower her hand moved against him, his kisses became more desperate. She could taste his hunger for her as his lips devoured hers.

His hands had worked the buttons of her dress undone, and he pulled it down over her shoulders. His lips left hers to wander to the curve of her neck. There, he placed soft kisses as his hands pulled her breasts free. The open air hit them, causing her nipples to tighten from the cool air floating off the sea.

Charles traced his finger over her shoulder to her breast. His finger burned a trail around the tight bud of her nipple. His lips followed his finger, and when he pulled at her nipple, Raina whimpered. Her hand stilled on his cock as she waited for his next move. When he drew her nipple in her mouth and sucked gently, Raina's hand tightened on his cock. As he sucked her harder, Raina stroked him harder. When his tongue flicked back and forth as he sucked, Raina stroked faster.

Charles sensed he was going to come out of his skin at this delicious torture. He began to kiss her other breast as his hand continued to tease her other nipple. His lips devoured her and brought her to a fevered pitch. Her hand stroked him faster and harder as he consumed her with kisses.

He needed to be inside her. His cock was growing harder and throbbing in her small palm. Her tight grip stroked him to a need of release.

Sliding his hand under her dress, he found her wet. His fingers slid inside her. She was ready for him. As his fingers glided in and out of her, her wetness coated his fingers. He wanted it to coat his cock. He increased the speed as he stroked her, only to have her do the same to him. His thumb found her clit and stroked her while she clenched around his fingers. Charles knew she was as close as he was to explosion.

As he rolled her over, he pulled her hands above her head and held them in one hand. Raina watched him as he slid himself inside her. She closed her eyes as he pushed in farther. Slowly. Making her experience every throbbing inch of him as he moved in deeper. He paused when he slid all the way in. She opened her eyes, begging him to move. He waited. She whimpered. Still, he waited. His body was shaking from the anticipation of Raina losing herself around him.

He pressed into her and moved his hips in small circles. She gasped and tried to move her hands. He tightened them and pressed into her again. He felt her tighten around his cock as her wetness coated them.

Raina wrapped her legs around his hips, needing to touch him any way she could. She knew she was unraveling around him, but he wanted more. More than she thought she could give. But still he persisted. Raina lifted her hips to him, drawing him in deeper. She tried to make him move against her. She needed him. When she moved her hips with his, he let out a growl. Charles let her hands go as he drove into her.

Raina pulled his head down to kiss him hungrily. She ran her fingers through his hair, her fingers gripping as he slid in and out of her. Raina matched him stroke for stroke as he made love to her. The power of their bodies as they pleasured each other became more powerful as they opened themselves to one another.

Charles pulled Raina closer to him and kissed her deeply as he felt her body surrender to him. In return, he gave himself to her, filling her with his love.

Rolling over, he pulled her close, covering them with the blanket. The touch of the cool breeze washed over their heated bodies, cooling them with a gentle touch.

Chapter Sixteen

RAINA HELD ONTO HIS hand as they made their way back to the cottage. Neither one of them had spoken since making love. She felt a new and unspoken connection with Charles. It was too new and raw for either of them to explore. Raina kept from telling Charles how she cared for him, afraid it could shatter. She realized their time here was ending. Wherever their paths took them, would this feeling stay this strong, or would it weaken? Raina now understood that in order to survive she had to put her trust in Charles. She needed to open herself to this vulnerability. The vulnerability of loving somebody other than herself.

She looked up when Charles squeezed her hand. Raina stared into his eyes and saw what she felt. He appeared to understand her inner struggle and wanted her to know he was there for her. She smiled her appreciation at him. He squeezed her hand tighter and pulled her into his embrace. They stood along the path and watched as the sun rested against the sparkling blue water, its orange rays dipping their tips into the water, cooling off after a fulfilling day exploring life.

He tugged on her hand and led her along the garden path. His arm wrapped around her waist as they walked inside the cottage. Hearing an unfamiliar voice coming from the kitchen, their feet led them toward the sound of the uninvited guest. Upon entering, they saw Maxwell seated at the small table with Mrs. Hobbs, sharing a pot of tea. He sat there charming the elderly lady as he ate away at the cake, gossiping, unaware of their presence.

"You don't say, Mrs. Hobbs. Married, is he? Well, we didn't see that happening, did we? What is the new bride like? Charming, I imagine?" he asked the caretaker.

"Oh, she is such a dear. She has worked on bringing the gardens back to their magnificent glory since we lost the duchess. Charles is so smitten with her and follows her around like a puppy dog."

Maxwell laughed at the picture that described the happy couple. He had seen them enter the room out of the corner of his eye but kept Mrs. Hobbs chatting about them.

Turning in his seat, he lifted the fork in the air, "I hear congratulations are in order, my friend." Sliding the fork between his lips, he ate the sweet confection.

"Delicious as always, Mrs. Hobbs."

Mrs. Hobbs blushed at his praise. She came to her feet, bustling around the kitchen, looking busy. She should not have been gossiping, but she was thrilled for the couple and was glad to have somebody to share it with besides Mr. Hobbs. While Mr. Hobbs spoke few words, he also was one to only want to hear few words spoken to him in return.

Charles pulled Raina to his side, holding her tightly. There was only one reason Maxwell was in Dover, and it wasn't good. He kept a hold on her, for fear of her fleeing. He felt her tense as soon as they came upon their guest. Her mind was working on twenty different ways she could make her escape. But if she thought he would let her out of his sight, she had another thing coming. Now that he had found her, she wasn't going anywhere.

Charles dropped the picnic basket on the table, rattling the plates. Turning to Mrs. Hobbs, he thanked her for the delightful picnic and made their excuses. He nodded his head at their uninvited guest to follow them.

Making his way to the library, he kept a tight hold on Raina. He was sending her the message of their unity, and he would not let her go.

After he shut the door, he led Raina to the settee. Once she was settled, he turned toward their guest.

"To what do we owe the pleasure of this visit, Maxwell?"

He watched as his friend settled into a chair opposite from Raina, smirking as he watched them.

"Had I known of your nuptials, I would have brought a token for the celebration. But alas, I have nothing to give," he said as he patted at his clothes.

"How did you learn where we were?"

"This was the only safe place you could come with nobody besides your family knowing your whereabouts. Well, family and a close friend, anyhow."

"Were you followed?"

"Tell me, why do you risk your life and your family's lives for this piece of baggage? A lady who, for the right price, could end your very existence in a heartbeat?"

Charles lunged at Maxwell, his fist connecting to his face. Charles grabbed him by the lapels of his jacket and threw him from the chair. He was bending over to punch him in the gut when he heard the cocking of the pistol. As he looked down, he saw the barrel of the gun aimed at his stomach. When he glanced back up, he saw how serious his friend was. Or the chap who used to be his friend. He heard Raina gasp as she saw the gun pointed at him.

"I commend you on your display of affection for the lady. With your display of defending her honor, I now understand your feelings. But what I wonder is if she feels the same way for you?"

Maxwell waved the pistol, motioning for Charles to rise. As Charles backed away from him, Maxwell came to his feet with the pistol still aimed at Charles.

"Why are you doing this?" Charles asked. Everybody's doubts about his friend were starting to ring true. His actions were now pointed to where his allegiances were.

"So, do they, madam? Or should I say Lady Mallory? Will you risk your life for him? If I were to pull the trigger," Maxwell cocked the pistol again, "and take my aim," he raised the pistol to Mallory's heart, "what will you do?" Maxwell asked as his finger started to release from the trigger.

Raina watched in horror as Maxwell pointed the gun at Charles. He was spouting utter nonsense about honor. All she thought of was losing him. In the short time they had been together, Raina now realized he was her world. There was no greater gentleman than the one before her. He was her heart. She didn't even ponder what her actions would be; her heart knew what to do. As she watched Maxwell releasing his finger on the trigger, she cried out as she jumped in front of Charles, protecting his body with hers.

Charles hands gripped Raina's arms as she threw her body in the path of the bullet. He tried to move her body out of the way, but she fought against him to save his life. Raina waited for the echo of the bullet to release into the small library. Her body tensed for the invasion, waiting for the pain to engulf her. The only thing that happened was the clank of the hammer hitting the firing pin.

No smoke. No noise. No pain. Only the sight of a deranged earl sliding the pistol back into his pocket, then making a bow toward them. As Maxwell staggered over to the bar cart, he poured himself a shot of whiskey. Throwing it back quickly, he poured himself another. As he clutched the decanter, he settled on the settee, throwing his legs across the cushions. He tipped his glass to Mallory.

"Congratulations, Mallory. It seems she feels the same way you do," Maxwell slurred.

Only then did Charles see his friend was drunk. He only acted as he did to see where Raina's loyalties laid. His actions were a test for Raina, to see which side she fought for. While it was inexcusable, Charles understood. He meant no real harm. There was an underlying message as to why Maxwell behaved in this manner. But as he watched his friend continue to drink, he knew he would not get his answers now.

"Your smashed," Raina said.

"You are correct in that assumption, Lady Mallory," Maxwell answered as he slid his arm over his eyes.

Raina stood, glowering in her frustration. When he showed no sign of remorse for his actions, she turned to Charles for his response. It was when he shrugged his shoulders at her and moved the decanter from Maxwell's hand and took a drink for himself that she became furious. She growled her aggravation at the two men as she stormed from the room.

"Are you going to follow her?"

"It would be in my best interest if I don't at this time."

"She is a feisty lady; your life will be adventuresome with her."

"Yes, I am aware," Charles answered with a smile of contentment.

Maxwell rolled his eyes at the demise of his single friend. While he was thrilled for the couple, he recognized the danger ahead for them. He hoped the love he witnessed between them could endure the risk.

"Don't worry, old chap. Got rid of the followers along the trail," Maxwell mumbled before exhaustion took hold.

~~~~~~~

Charles sat and waited for his friend to awaken. Friend or enemy? Charles was not quite sure which. All he noticed was the fellow before him was a wreck. He had never seen his friend like this, passed out drunk. Especially when he needed to be on his toes. Nightfall had come and gone, and now the early morning sun was trying to peek out upon the horizon. Still, he did not leave his side. There had to be a reason for Maxwell to track him to the cottage. The only question that remained was if his friend could be trusted.

Hearing him groan, Charles shifted his eyes toward the settee. He watched as Maxwell stretched and wiped the gritty sleep from his eyes. He did not move from the chair. When Maxwell's eyes met his, he raised his eyebrows in the usual sardonic eyebrow raise he was famous for. When Mallory responded with one of his own, Maxwell let out a long sigh.

"You owe her an apology," Charles said.

"I know, but I needed to see."

"You already saw. You were only trying to prove a point."

Maxwell shrugged at the comment and responded, "Maybe."

"Why are you here?"

"Supposed to bring her back to Shears. He has a nice bounty on her head."

"Over my dead body."

"Yes, that is what I informed him you would say, old chap."

"And what was his response?"

"To do whatever I had to do. Kill you both, if I must."

"Then what's stopping you?"

"I don't know anymore."

"What does he have on you, Maxwell?"

"He has information about what I want."

"What information? I think you are working a different mission than the one assigned to us."

"It is personal."

"As in?"

"As in, none of your concern. I am only here to warn you, so you can vanish with your new wife and hide until I can take care of Shears."

"We have no intention of hiding from that man. Raina and I will journey to London tonight. I have just received word from Thorn that it is safe to return."

"You are writing your own death sentence if you return."

"No, my friend, you are as long as you keep aligning yourself with him."

Maxwell rose from the settee and walked over to the windows. When he lifted the curtains, he searched for any sign of danger. He had been trailed here. While he had removed those followers, he knew more would come. Shears had men everywhere who kept track of everybody's moves. Nobody was safe from him.

"You need to move Raina out of here today. I got rid of Shears's men, but more will follow."

"I know. We are leaving at nightfall."

"We need to make it look like I have killed you."

"I think we can figure something out."

Maxwell nodded and continued to watch out the window. Mallory realized he was not going to confide in him. As close as they were, Maxwell always kept a part of himself shut off from his friends. His secrets were his own. While that was fine in the past, his secrets were putting every one of his friends in danger lately. Danger that caused mistakes to be made and lives put at risk.

"One day you will realize your friends are here for you. I only hope it will not be too late."

With those words, Mallory left the room. He had preparations to make for them to leave tonight. Also, he needed Mr. and Mrs. Hobbs to help him pull off a double homicide at the hands of Earl Zane Maxwell. After word reached London of their deaths at his hands, no London ballroom would be available as his hunting grounds. The inside of Newgate Prison would be his new home. He wanted to find Raina and calm her down. She never searched for him through the night after Maxwell passed out. He figured she was still angry with him.

~~~~~

Raina let herself in from her walk and strode by the library, still angry with both men inside the room. One for pulling the obnoxious prank and the other for allowing it. She was the angriest at Charles for not searching for her last evening. When she walked by, both doors were wide open. When she peeked her head inside, it was to find a deserted room.

As she walked through the small cottage, she tried to search out Charles but only came up empty. She never even ran across Mrs. Hobbs. She climbed the stairs, deciding to retire to her room. When she opened the door, she found Maxwell stretched out in the chair before the fire, reading the book she had been reading the night before. Closing the door, she advanced on him and slapped him across the face. He grabbed her hand after she struck him. His fingers lightly held her wrist.

"I will allow you one and only one."

"You deserve more."

Maxwell nodded. "Correct as always, my dear, but nonetheless that is all you will have."

Raina jerked her wrist out of his hold and walked to the window.

"I hear you have given him doubt on my character."

Raina spun from the window. "That is the plan, is it not? To cause doubt about your allegiances?"

Maxwell sighed. "That is the plan." His voice sounded weary.

"I have not gone through everything I have gone through for you to give up now."

"Don't make it sound as if it has all been horrific, my dear. From my view yesterday afternoon, you appeared to be enjoying yourself immensely."

"You scoundrel, I see peeping should be listed with your crimes."

"It is not peeping when you're out on display for anybody to witness."

"Have you no shame, sir?"

"Oh, I have plenty, as you are well aware."

Raina made an humphing sound as she turned to her belongings. Searching through her things she threw the contents of her bag across the bed. As she searched she asked him, "I suppose you are here for the jewels?"

"That is one reason I am in your bedroom."

"And the other reasons?" she inquired.

"Why to kill you and Mallory, of course." He responded as if they were discussing the weather. Plain and simple and to the point.

She paused and raised her eyes to him. To gage the truth behind his words. But, as always, Maxwell hid his emotions behind his calm façade. His eyes wouldn't give him away, for they never did. Raina dug deeper into her bag, wrapping her hand around the knife she kept hidden. While she had her doubts about trusting Maxwell, he had saved her life many times over the course of the last few months. While trusting was hard for her to do, he had proven to be an ally. But she had seen the other side—the side his friends had not. The side that showed whether he could be trusted. Whose side he was truly on.

She was the only one who knew of his special mission. It was one she was forced to join before revenge had overtaken her life. She kept his secret because it kept her alive with the Crown. Raina was a spy who was knowledgeable of both sides. But the Crown thought she could be of more valuable use to them, so they applauded her revenge because it kept their hands from being soiled.

"Drop the knife, Raina, and hand over the jewels. I have searched your bag and the room, so quit playing me false. I have come to do a job, and I will succeed in doing it. We can either do this my way or we can do it yours. Which will it be?"

Raina only tightened her grip on the knife. She assessed her position and knew Charles would come to her rescue if they struggled. Not that she needed him to. She was trained to take down bigger men than Maxwell. However, by the state of Maxwell's behavior, she knew Mallory's aid would be much appreciated.

"I gather you have chosen by the look in your eyes. I mean you no harm."

"You are threatening to murder us."

"No, I am merely stating my mission, and that is to kill you."

"One and the same."

"No, my mission is to execute you, but how the mission plays out and how it is perceived are different."

Raina pulled her hand out of the bag and held the knife in front of her in defense.

"Explain yourself."

"I will as soon as you hand over the jewels."

Raina could not hand him what he sought. Her jewelry box was not in her bag. While the box looked to be an innocent young girl's trinket, it was anything but. The secret compartment held the jewels Maxwell spoke of—jewels she was to safeguard. In her hurry to leave the Thornhills', she must have left them behind. She only hoped they would not be found in her absence. She could never forgive herself if those jewels fell into the wrong hands. They were the only thing keeping a young charge from becoming another one of Shears's victims.

"I am unable to at this time."

"Explain yourself," Maxwell growled as he came forward to sit on the edge of the chair. His nonchalant manner disappeared at this bit of news.

"I am afraid I have misplaced them, but I know where they are." Raina held out her hand to stop him after he came out of the chair toward her.

"Where?" he demanded.

"Hillston House."

"Damn it, Raina," he roared. While the coarse language was rough to any other lady's ears, it was not to hers. She had heard worse, especially in the last few months. While she was considered a lady at one time, she was no longer. Even if she aspired to be, this war made it impossible for what she most desired.

As rapidly as he had come at her, he retraced his steps, slumping back into the chair. Only this time he didn't slouch as if he had not a care in the universe. Instead, he slumped in defeat. Leaning forward, he ran his fingers through his hair over and over. Then finally he leaned back with his head lying against the cushion of the chair and closed his eyes. Raina could see the fight leaving his body.

"The Thornhill residence is as safe a location as any."

"How so?"

"Ivy will keep it safe for me. I trust she will. If they open it, they will only find my trinkets. The jewels are hidden in a secret compartment," Raina explained.

"There is only one problem."

"What could that be?"

"Thornhill holds the red ruby as well."

Finally, Raina realized the depth of Maxwell's desperation. The reason he was acting like a crazed man. Without those jewels he lost all leverage in his search. The search could end Shears and every man involved. They needed to retrieve those jewels from Thornhill. While those jewels were in his possession, it only brought danger to his family. While he was unaware of the risk, it was only a matter of time before danger would be upon them. What had she done? She unknowingly brought chaos to Charles's family. Would he ever forgive her? Now was not the time to wonder. They needed to act as soon as possible.

"I will sneak in and retrieve the jewels, and then you can carry out the mission."

"The jewels are not my only mission, Raina. I was sent here to murder you and Mallory, and that is precisely what I will do."

Before Raina could react, Maxwell was upon her. He peeled the knife from her fingers and pulled her in his grasp. Raina fought against his hold, but she was no match for his strength. She let out a scream to wake the dead; it was her only weapon left. She only hoped Charles was near.

"Yes, continue to scream. This way I will not have to search for him. He will come to your rescue," Maxwell urged her on.

Raina clamped her lips shut. But it was too late. Charles rushed into the room in her defense. Only this time Maxwell had his gun aimed at her instead.

Chapter Seventeen

CHARLES HAD SEARCHED THE cottage and grounds for Raina. When he could not find her, he decided to wait for her return in her bedroom. As he came upon her room, it was to find the door closed and hushed voices beyond the door.

When he pressed his ear against the door, he listened to Raina and Maxwell. The only argument he overheard was missing jewels. They were quite familiar with each other. Too familiar actually. There was more to their relationship than he realized. Were they working together? Was Raina still involved with Shears? Impossible. Her anger toward the man was as plain as day. Or was it all a cover-up to throw everybody off their game? Listening closer, he heard the desperation in both of their voices. When he heard them arguing, he realized he needed to help her. Before he entered the bedroom, Raina let out a screech loud enough to bring everybody in the house to her rescue. But no sooner had she belted it out, the shriek stopped.

Charles shoved the door open to rescue her. Only this time it was Raina who was at the end of Maxwell's gun, not him. He came to a halting stop before them. When he glanced at Raina, he noticed the small shake of her head and the look in her eyes telling him to back away. But he also recognized the fear, fear only he could see. Charles lowered his hands and backed away and turned his stare to Maxwell. What he saw there surprised him most. It was the look of a desperate man willing to go as far as he must to achieve the results he needed.

"Killing us will not gain you what you think it will," Mallory tried to reason.

"It will get me one step closer."

"Shears will not fulfill what he has promised you. You are only performing his dirty work for him."

"Not this time."

"We can work together and figure out a different solution. I promise I will help you find whatever you are searching for."

"He is the only one with the information I seek."

"Let me help you, friend."

Maxwell scoffed at the word. "Friend? Do you really think I believe you still consider me a friend after everything I have done to you?"

Mallory only had one word for him, regardless of whether he trusted him. "Yes."

This only made Maxwell laugh. It was a deranged laugh that only a desperate man would give when he ran out of options. He believed Mallory meant it, or thought he meant it, but Maxwell knew better. There was only one way to end this, and it was to kill them and retrieve the jewels from Thornhill. Afterward, he could present himself to Shears with the jewels and the news of Charles and Raina's death.

He waved his gun at Mallory and motioned for him to take a seat in the chair. When Mallory complied, he thrust Raina away from him and moved to the door. After he shut the door, he walked toward them, where Mallory had risen from the chair and pushed Raina behind him.

"This is not what I want to do. You must understand killing both of you is my last hope," Maxwell pleaded with them.

"We understand your desperation, Zane, but there must be another way."

"No, this is my final opportunity with Shears. If I do not show him my loyalty, he will have me killed, and then I cannot complete my mission. Then our existence as we understand it will change, and not for the better."

"But your mission will be complete when we bring Shears and the men who support him to justice."

"There is no justice with greed and corruption, my friend."

"There will be."

"That is not my only mission, Mallory."

"What are you talking about?"

"Why don't you ask the new Lady Mallory?"

"Why would Raina have knowledge of your mission?"

Maxwell laughed at them. "Not yet sharing secrets while lying among the bed pillows?"

Mallory turned to Raina for an explanation. She backed away from them, turning her back as she put more distance between them, making her way over to the door.

"Not so fast," Maxwell said, stopping her.

"Raina?" Charles questioned.

Raina turned toward the men, scowling at Maxwell. "Damn you."

"Tsk, tsk, such language for a lady. But then you are not a true lady are you, my dear."

Raina's anger got the better of her, and she advanced on him, slapping him across the face, which only made Maxwell continue to laugh at her more. He had put her in a position where she had to continue to lie to Charles. She could not betray her cover, and he realized her dilemma. He was an utter bastard. She recognized the only way out of this mess was to continue her lies. Lies that were building more the longer she stayed with Charles. Lies that would crumble. She could only spin lies for so long before somebody figured them out. Even though her mind believed the lies, the truth always surfaced. And when it did, they would hurt the ones she loved the most.

Charles's hand reached out and turned her toward him. His eyes searched hers for any truth to Maxwell's lies. He could not tell what was in her gaze. The tension between she and Maxwell spoke of a deeper relationship than he was aware of. But her eyes swiftly concealed what she was thinking, let alone feeling. Was there honesty in Maxwell's words? He had a sense he would not find out while Maxwell was anywhere near them. He needed to get Raina alone to find out. But to do that, he had to get them out of there alive before Maxwell fell true to his own word and killed them both. He slid his hand along Raina's arm and held onto her hand, giving it a gentle squeeze. He conveyed his feelings of support to her, with no need for her to utter any more lies on what she kept from him. She looked up to him, and he noticed the look of surprise in her eyes at his acceptance.

Acceptance was hard for Raina to understand. How did Charles not question her for what Maxwell was saying? But then it was Charles, always understanding to the final word. His faith in her was new to her. Not since her father had anybody had this much understanding or belief in her. Raina finally realized the depth of his feelings for her in this one simple act. The pressure of his hand against hers explained his thoughts. As she gazed into his eyes, she saw it all. It overwhelmed her, but she understood. She gave a small nod of her head and closed her eyes at his affection. When she opened them again, it was to see what she had been missing all along. A soft smile touched her lips. A smile that spoke to him, she hoped. When she saw his return smile, she knew he understood. Their unspoken connection made her smile grow wider. A small laugh escaped her lips.

"Why are you two smiling and laughing? Do you not comprehend your fate?" Maxwell growled.

Raina turned back toward Maxwell and watched as he shook the pistol at them, his hand shaking. She saw the signs and realized it would happen in a matter of minutes. Minutes she could talk her way through. Express with just enough words to make him wonder where she stood.

"Why yes, Lord Maxwell. I completely understand my fate and the fate of those I love."

"Oh, you think you have found love?"

Smiling over at Charles, she whispered, "Yes." Then turning toward Maxwell, she spoke louder. "Yes, I have found love. Love I will not let you destroy with your ranting."

"Ranting you know to be true. It will only be a matter of time before your love knows them too."

Maxwell lowered himself onto the edge of the bed. He felt light-headed suddenly, and arguing with Raina only made him become more unfocused. His mission needed to end, and if he could carry out his mission, he could be on his way. His nerves were making him sick to his stomach. This wasn't how he wanted to end his friendship with Mallory, but it was the only way. Wiping the sweat from his forehead, he closed his eyes briefly to remove the black spots that had appeared before his eyes. As he heard Raina prattle on about her loyalties, he tried to stop the ringing in his ears. He heard movement, and his eyes tried to focus on the two figures before him. The only thing he was making out were two blurs wavering in front of him. Closing his eyes again and openly them rapidly only made matters worse. A wave of dizziness overtook him. He felt himself passing out onto the mattress. As his head hit the soft counterpane, his last thought was of his failure.

Raina gradually inched toward Maxwell, her smile growing wider as she watched the drugs finally overtake him. They sure took their time taking him out. He had no idea what hit him. She suffered no remorse for what she did, only a sense of relief in escaping this dilemma. She knew he would try again, but by then hopefully they could convince him of an alternative route. He was desperate, and that drove him to this behavior. Soon she would have to come clean with Charles on her involvement with Maxwell. If not, Charles would have Maxwell locked up for treason. If that happened, then Shears would escape justice. Then it would only give him more power than he already had. Doing so would risk the mission Maxwell needed to complete. But it could also make sure every one of their missions failed, as well as jeopardize the safety of England and the Crown.

"I suppose this is the work of you drugging him?" Charles asked from behind her.

She watched him as he walked around the side of the bed and eased the gun out of Maxwell's hand. Charles laid the gun on the stand by the bed, then threw Maxwell's legs on the bed. Standing over his friend, he watched him with a frown on his face. He turned toward her and waited for her explanation.

Shrugging her shoulders, she answered, "I might have helped him with his much-needed rest."

"The same way you helped me a few weeks ago?"

"Both of you had it coming to you. If not for drugging him, we would be the ones lying there, dead I might say."

"He was not going to kill us, Raina."

"He was too. You might not want to accept this about your friend, but he is more than capable of murdering us."

"No, he's not. It was an act, an act that has now put us in a quandary."

"I don't understand."

"No, I don't suppose you do. But then we all have our secrets don't we, darling?"

"It appears we do."

"I will share mine if you want to share yours."

"I have no secrets you would be interested in. But feel free to share yours."

"Oh, you have many secrets I would be fascinated in, my dear. But feel free to keep them. I will always be here when you are ready to share them. As for mine, they are simple. Maxwell shared with me why he was here and what he was to accomplish. We came up with a plan for us to make our way back to London undetected and for him to carry back news to Shears of our demise. But as you can grasp now, the act has changed. May I inquire how long he will be out?"

Raina winced. "Tomorrow morning."

Charles sighed and sank onto the mattress beside his friend. As he sat there, he tried to figure out their options. The plan was for Maxwell to shoot them with blanks and for Hobbs to find them covered in blood, where they would spread word in the village of their deaths. Maxwell would then load them in the wagon and transport them back to London, where word of their deaths would spread among the ton. Then Maxwell was going to report back to Shears of their demise and finish his mission. Charles did not ask what his mission was. The less he knew at this point the safer he could keep his family and Raina. But for this mission to succeed, they needed to move in the dead of night. Now they were unable to. Before long, the thugs that followed Maxwell would find them. Then none of them would be safe. He didn't want to involve the Hobbs in this anymore then he already was, so Mr. Hobbs driving them to London was out of the question.

Feeling tired suddenly, he lay back on the mattress. The late nights and worrying had left him exhausted. He closed his eyes and tried to consider of a way out of this mess. Shaking away the light-headedness, he opened his eyes. When he saw the room in a haze, he realized it was not exhaustion, but that she had drugged him too. Pulling himself up to a sitting position, he focused on her across the room. The guilt on her face was evidence enough of what she achieved with them.

"Why?" he asked her.

"Why what?"

"Did you have to drug me too?"

She looked at him in confusion. "I did not drug you, Charles. Only Maxwell."

"No more lies, Raina," his words slurred.

Raina rushed toward him when she realized what he was implying.

"I am not lying, Charles. Please have faith in me."

"No more—" he muttered as he passed out next to his friend.

"Charles," Raina shouted as she shook him.

But he was not going to awaken any more than his friend next to him. Fools, both of them. They needed to leave at once. There was no time to waste. She needed to put into action her own plan for their return to London. Never leave it to a man to complete what needed to be done. It was the one thing her mother had engrained into her. Raina went over to the wardrobe and loaded her portmanteau with her belongings. As she packed her bag, she looked again for the missing jewelry box, but it was not to be found. She only hoped it was still with the Thornhills.

Raina turned at the sound of the door opening and watched as Mrs. Hobbs came inside, wringing her hands nervously. She watched as Raina filled her bag with her clothing, looking over at the two gentlemen lying on the bed.

"I am so sorry, My Lady. I tried to stop him from eating the cake. But he was questioning me on Lord Maxwell, and I did not want to look suspicious. I tried to warn you, but I could not locate you."

"It is okay, Mrs. Hobbs. I figured that was the case when he passed out a few moments ago. We will have to change to plan B now. Since Charles is unable to help me and he will be out as long as Maxwell, I will have to transport us back to London by myself."

"You will not be safe traveling through the darkness."

"I have no other choice. We have to leave tonight before the men who were trailing Maxwell find us. It won't be long before they do."

"Which is why you will let us help you. Our nephew Billy will drive the cart, and you will hide in the back with the men. He will spread the story of your demise along the way. Mr. Hobbs and I will spread the lies around the village. By morning, the news will have spread along with you to London. There will be no doubt left in anybody's mind of the tragic end to your poorly departed lives. It was a tragic end. A lovers' spat gone wrong. With you caught in the middle between the two men who loved you, but only one man who you had given your heart to." Tears fell down her cheeks with the story she weaved.

Raina blinked at the sorrow the woman was displaying. The housekeeper should have acted on stage with the performance she was giving. It appeared she wasn't the only woman with a plan. Shaking her head with a smile, she reached to hug the stout woman. Drawing her plump body in her arms, she thanked her for everything, but mostly for her acceptance of her. With everything the woman was doing for her, she could not leave with the lie weighing heavy on her heart.

"We are not really married."

"I know, my dear, but it is only a temporary issue, one which will be remedied as soon as you two find the time."

"I am not so sure anymore."

"I am never wrong, my dear. The man adores you, and you him. You will bring me little ones to watch run in the charming garden you brought back to life. Mark my words."

Raina said no more. It wasn't necessary to argue with dreams that were not meant to be. It was best left to let Mrs. Hobbs believe in fantasy. They needed to leave. As she glanced around the room, she drew her memories inside her heart. She would reflect on her time at this cottage and how it healed her soul later.

Chapter Eighteen

THE CART HIT EVERY bump and rut in the road. If they were not flying at a breakneck speed, the wagon crept along the uneven terrain. Raina squished between the two sleeping gentlemen and felt pinned in the cramp space. Her headache was only made worse by both men snoring in each of her ears. She rolled her eyes at the sound. As the cart settled into a groove in the road and became a smoother ride, Raina's exhaustion took hold. She curled on her side to face Charles. After adjusting her eyes to the dark, she regarded him as he slept. She had spent more moments with him sleeping or sick than she had with him awake. During times like this, she experienced the most security with him. It was perhaps because she did not suffer from the guilt for every single lie and secret she kept from him.

Not that Charles wasn't secure during any other spell. He was. He made her feel safe and vulnerable in a good way, which gave her the sense of a lady loved by her man. Not any gentleman, but the man she loved in return. She knew she had much to answer for when he woke. Also, she realized it would be time for her to share with him her total involvement with Shears, Maxwell, and the mission assigned to her by the Crown.

Raina kissed him lightly on the forehead then snuggled next to him for warmth and drifted off to sleep with her head pressed against his shoulder.

Charles saw the exact second Maxwell came out of his drug-induced sleep. He had been watching him and waiting. He had woken a while ago, feeling the drug leave his body and sharpen his awareness of his surroundings. His eyes adjusted to the dark, cramped space to see when his enemy would awake. He noticed the woman curled into his side, with her head lying trustingly on his shoulder. He had gazed at her for a short time, his anger at her gradually creeping away as the cart took them to their destination. She had to quit drugging him. If she only trusted him, they could have worked something out together. Granted, he had not trusted her in return with his and Maxwell's plan of escape. He recognized now where he had erred. From here on out, he promised to include her on every plan.

He considered Maxwell an enemy now because he had deviated from their plan. In no part of their scheme was he to hold a gun to Raina. He took it too far; it was at that moment when he realized the true danger they were in with Maxwell. Raina had been right the entire time. Maxwell had his own agenda, and it was not to see to their safety. Could he really have killed them for Shears? He would not give him a chance to find out.

While he kept his eye on Maxwell, he knew the man was tied up, his arms pulled behind his back. Maxwell struggled to wake, shaking his hair out of his eyes. When Maxwell turned his head to search his surroundings, his eyes landed on his. He noticed the moment the other man realized he was trapped and no longer in control. While his gaze first held confusion, it rapidly turned to anger. Maxwell let out a low growl, and he struggled with his bound hands.

"Lie still, Maxwell. You are not going anywhere."

"Where are we headed?"

"I do not know."

"What do you mean, you don't know?"

"It appears my lovely wife here drugged us, bound you, and has set us on to our destination."

"Well wake your lovely wife and find out." Maxwell's voice dripped with sarcasm.

Mallory looked upon the sleeping Raina and back to Maxwell. "I think not."

Maxwell growled his annoyance at the spot of trouble he was in. Lying still, he quit struggling against the rope binding his hands together. He had panicked when he woke in the dark. He thought Shears had him, but when his eyes adjusted to find Mallory watching him, he figured he was safe. For now, anyhow. But he was still in a dilemma. He was no closer to getting the jewels and completing his mission than he was in running on this fool's errand of killing Charles and Raina. Oh, he had no intention of killing them, just acting like he did. Enough to fool Shears into giving him the last piece of the puzzle he needed. Now he was stuck in a cart riding to who the hell knew where, with the same two targets who were supposed to be dead. He needed to get himself out of this mess and rethink a new plan.

"Why?" Charles asked him unexpectedly.

Maxwell shrugged his shoulders. He understood what Mallory was asking, and he had no intention of answering. He was a desperate man. And desperate men did desperate things. One of those was holding a gun on his friend's "wife." He snorted. They were no more married than he was innocent of the charges they held against him. He realized he was wrong to have threatened Raina. He owed her an apology, but of all folks, she would understand the most of why he did what he did. They shared a kinship in this war. He would apologize one day when this ended. For now, his friend would have to stay angry with him. It was better that way. The more distance they kept, the safer he would be.

"Answer me, damn you," Charles snarled in anger.

But Maxwell did not offer him any explanation, which only made Mallory angrier. He wanted to wipe the smug arrogance off his face. Maxwell showed no remorse for his actions. If anything, he smirked. As soon as this cart stopped, Mallory would make sure he understood the full brush of his anger. He would make sure Maxwell was held accountable for his actions. His only hope was that Raina was transporting them to Thornhill. He trusted her instincts. Thornhill could help him make sure Maxwell came clean with them.

Raina stirred in his arms. Their harsh whispers and the tightening of his arms around her woke her. When her body stretched and her eyes blinked open, he was trapped in her stare. So caught up in her gaze, he did not see Maxwell had untied his hands. When he caught movement out of the corner of his eye, he jerked his gaze back to Maxwell and saw him getting ready to climb over the side of the cart.

Maxwell turned back in time to glare at Mallory, nodding his head. "Until another day, my friend."

With those words, he stared as Maxwell jumped out of the wagon. Swearing, he let go of Raina and moved to the back of the cart, where he saw Maxwell landing on the dirt road. Maxwell picked himself up and ran into the woods, the dark night embracing his shadows as he drifted away. As he got ready to follow him, he kicked his legs off the end of the wagon. A hand reached out to stop him, pulling him away from the edge.

"Let him go, Charles."

"After what he did to you? No, he will pay for threatening you."

"He would never shoot. We both believe he would never harm either one of us."

"You are being too merciful."

"You have taught me to forgive."

Charles was silent with her confession. She wanted him to forgive Maxwell for his crimes. The tables were now turned. How could he turn against what he preached if he wasn't willing to do the same? Sighing, he let her pull him from the edge. He knew she was correct.

"He will be back, Charles, and you will have your answers soon enough."

"Even the ones you still hold so dear?"

Lowering her head, she nodded. "Even those."

Raina wanted to share her secrets with Charles, but now wasn't the time. The cart was slowing. They would enter London soon. Shortly they would play their biggest role yet. There was only a small measure of time to explain her plan to Charles.

She told Charles her idea, and he agreed it was workable. They agreed the plan of surprise only made it more believable. It would hurt and scare the ones he loved, but only for a short while. Only long enough to fool everybody in their deaths. They needed only one person to hear of their death being told to Charles's family, and word would spread among the ton like wildfire. If the ton shared the gossip, then eventually word would spread to Shears. Raina convinced Charles that Maxwell might have a chance at completing his mission. It was a small lie, one she could remedy as soon as she was able. She knew it was only one step closer for Maxwell to complete. The missing jewels were the final step. One he would have to invade the Thornhills' to accomplish. He wasn't a mad man to invade the townhome. Or was he?

Chapter Nineteen

ONCE THE CART HAD slowed to a stop, they realized it was their time
to put on the performance they'd planned. Charles had whispered the plan to
Billy as they headed into London. They agreed it was Billy who would
inform the Thornhills' butler, Sims, of their demise. Sims would inform
Thorn. Billy would tell Sims he could bring the bodies into the residence,
where they could sneak in undetected. They hoped Ivy would be
entertaining callers for afternoon tea when Sims told the sad tale.

The cart shook as Billy jumped off and ran to the door meant for the
servants. He pounded against the rough slate. A downstairs maid answered,
whereupon Billy asked to see Sims at once. The young maid argued at his
demands, but when Billy whispered why he needed to see him, the maid
burst into tears and ran from the door. They listened to her cry for help.
Once Sims arrived at the back door, Billy told him the sad tale Mrs. Hobbs
had construed. Sims was in shock and gave Billy directions to move the
bodies around back and through a private entrance. He was instructed to
take the servants' stairs and to leave the bodies in a bedroom. Sims told
Billy that he would need to explain Charles and Raina's deaths to Lord
Thornhill.

Billy navigated the cart around to the back entrance. When he lifted
the tarp, Charles whispered for him to take Raina first. He did not want to
leave Raina vulnerable in the open cart. He could protect himself better.
Billy swung Raina up into his arms. Charles smiled as he watched her

perform. Nobody played dead better than her. Her body went limp in the young man's arms, her head swaying back and forth. Charles saw the shock in Billy's eyes at the believability of her performance. Billy looked back at him in shock, where Charles only shook his head, smiled, and mouthed that she was acting. Billy gave a quick nod in understanding and carried her inside. Charles lay back and waited for Billy to come back to him. It didn't take long for him to return. It was a good thing Billy was a strapping young man built for labor, for when he lifted Charles, he did not do it so delicately, but instead threw him over his shoulder, clasping his arm around the back of Charles's legs. Raina was carried with care. He was being carried like a sack of potatoes. So much for being a privileged aristocrat. I guess it did not matter if you were dead or pretending to be dead. While Billy carried him through the private entrance, Charles could hear the grief spreading throughout the house. The plan seemed to be working.

Billy carried Charles into the room chosen for him. His body lay next to Raina on the bed. She continued her acting, lying as still as possible on the counterpane.

"I have to meet with Lord Thornhill in his private study for a full account of your deaths," Billy whispered to Mallory.

"Do so swiftly. Make your speech loud enough for the servants to listen to the news. Then inform Thornhill he needs to attend the bodies before Lady Ivy and send him here at once," Mallory whispered back.

"Yes, My Lord." Billy left the bedroom and closed the door.

They could not move or make a sound until the coast was clear and Thorn came to investigate their deaths. So, all he did was reach across to hold Raina's hand. Their fingers laced together, he gently squeezed her hand while she responded with her own softer squeeze. They lay in wait for the word of their deaths to spread. No sound came from outside the door. The house had an eerie silence upon it. Charles knew by now Ivy would have learned of his demise. He only hoped it brought no harm to the child she was carrying. Her sadness wouldn't be forever, only long enough for the plan to succeed.

~~~~~~

Thornhill listened to the tale Billy Hobbs was telling him. Something wasn't right about the story. The boy spoke too loudly for such horrible news. It was when Billy kept darting his eyes to the footmen that he understood. Charles and Raina were not dead, but only acting like they were. Thorn dismissed his footmen and waited for them to leave the room. Once the door was shut, he moved around in front of his desk. Leaning against the edge, he sized up Billy's character. Billy relaxed in his chair once they were alone in the room. The young man wiped his hands along the front of his pants. After the boy let out a long sigh, Thorn realized how nervous he had been.

"Will you please see to them at once, My Lord?" Billy asked.

"I will once my wife has been informed."

"Will you not look at them first?"

"Lady Ivy is having tea with a few ladies of the ton. I think telling her of her brother's death, her friends could comfort her. Do you not agree informing her would be wiser?"

Billy thought of the plan he had made with Lord Mallory and recognized for it to work, other members of society needed to hear of their deaths. He only hated for Lady Ivy to suffer when she did not need to. She had always been so kind to him whenever she visited the cottage; he hated for her to suffer any grief. But for this to succeed, they must follow the plan.

In the meantime, he needed for Lord Thornhill to spread the word, then Lady Ivy could know the full truth. He nodded his head in understanding.

"I will have Sims prepare you a room, where you will wait until I send for you again. The fewer servants you encounter, the better."

"Yes, My Lord."

Thornhill rang for Sims. He gave instructions for Billy's room. He left the young man in the capable hands of his butler. He understood what he needed to do. While he felt the same empathy for his wife Billy had, he also knew this was a means to an end. And that was for gossip to spread. He could spare his wife's emotions soon enough.

Thorn made his way to the receiving parlor. There he encountered Ivy playing hostess to a room full of the most elite of the ton. He knew this would cause her enormous grief, but if it would accomplish what Charles had set out to do. He must make his wife cry.

As he walked into the room, Thorn moved to Ivy's side. A huge smile lit her face at his appearance. He overheard the other woman teetering about their love for each other and sighing into their teacups. When he joined Ivy on the settee, he pulled her hands in his. He watched her smile diminish to a frown.

"What is it, Thorn? Have you found out news of Charles?"

"Yes, my dear, I am afraid so."

Ivy paled at the tone of his voice, and her hands tightened in his.

"What?" she whispered.

"There was an incident, and Charles and his wife have been murdered."

He caught Ivy against his chest as she passed out in his arms at those words. He knew it was for the best that she reacted this way. There was less he had to explain about something he himself was not even privy to. He heard the news spread across the parlor. Charles. Wife. Death. The whispered words between the ladies sounded likes shouts from the rooftops. He glanced around the room as they gossiped among themselves. When his eyes met theirs, they would look away in guilt. Whatever Charles meant to do, it was working. Now he needed these ladies to leave, so he could tend to Ivy. Rising from the couch, he held Ivy in his arms. He bowed his head at the women.

"Please forgive me, ladies. I must see to my wife's comfort at once."

"Yes, Lord Thornhill, we will be on our way. Please let us convey our deepest regrets at this tragedy," Lady Drummond said.

Thorn nodded his head at her words and swept Ivy from the room. He took the stairs to their suite as fast as he could. Upon entering the room, he lay her on the bed. Sitting next to her, he wiped the hair from her face, urging her to wake. When her eyelids fluttered open and met his, he saw her profound sorrow at the loss of her brother. Tears filled her eyes.

"Charles?"

"That I do not know, my dear. I believe it is a ruse to confuse his enemies. I will call for Mabel to sit with you while I investigate this. In the meantime, stay calm until I can bring you word."

"He is alive then?"

"I cannot tell you yet, my dear, but there is a strong chance he is alive. Please rest and do not upset yourself or the babe," Thorn told her as he wrapped his hand over their child.

Ivy pressed her hand against Thorn's. They felt the baby kick at their touch. With Thorn's hand covering hers, Ivy was secure in the knowledge that her brother was still alive. She would feel his loss, and she did not. Just like before, she knew he was not dead.

"Please hurry and find out the truth. I will rest while you do. I promise." She sensed the tenderness of his care toward her while his lips caressed hers.

Thorn rose from the bed once Mabel entered the room. With one last glance at his wife, he left. Awaiting him in the hallway was Sims. He followed Sims to the floor above. As he ventured farther along the dark corridor, he doubted Charles was alive. Once outside the door, he waited for Sims to retreat. There was naught but a silence that greeted him. When he opened the door, it was to find the bodies of Charles and Raina lying peacefully on the bed. Did he misconstrue what Billy was trying to tell him? Would he have to tell Ivy he was wrong and her brother did not survive? But then he witnessed the tiniest of movements. Were their hands enclosed together? Wandering over to the bed, he saw what anybody would notice if they stood above them. Their chests rose in time with their breaths. Thorn thumped Charles on the shoulder in annoyance for the scare.

"Use the secret passageway and meet me in my suite in ten minutes," Thorn instructed them.

He then turned toward the door. Locking the door behind him, he informed Sims at the end of the hallway to post a footman at the locked room and to not let a soul inside. He then returned to Ivy. Once in his room, he dismissed Mabel. Soon his father-in-law, the Duke of Kempbell, joined them. Ivy pressed him for answers, but he told her to be patient and that all her questions would soon be answered. As they settled around the fire, the closed panel opened. Charles and Raina appeared out of the darkness. Cobwebs were clinging to their clothes and hair, but that did not stop Ivy from rushing to them in tears. Charles held her as she sobbed her relief. Raina stood back, feeling guilty for the angst Ivy was suffering. Charles led Ivy back to the settee and settled her next to Thorn. He then pulled Raina into their small group. He settled her in a chair and sat next to her, holding her hand. He wanted to make his feelings for Raina apparent to his family, and that she had his full support. When he saw no resistance from his family, he relaxed back into the chair.

"Let me offer my apologies for the ordeal we had to put you through. It was the only way our plan would work."

"Why don't you start at the beginning? I assume this has to do with Shears?" inquired the duke.

"And Maxwell," Charles responded.

"What is Zane's involvement with your scheme?" asked Ivy.

"Shears ordered him to kill us."

"I do not believe it." Ivy defended her friend.

"Well believe it, sister. He was sent to murder us for his own selfish reasons."

"There must be a misunderstanding."

"Misunderstanding?" Charles scoffed. "The man held a pistol point blank at not only me but Raina too. No, dear sister, it was no misunderstanding."

"Please explain, Charles, so we might understand what you two went through," Thorn urged.

Charles explained Maxwell's arrival and how the events spiraled out of control. Raina injected pieces of information along the way to support the story. Once they finished their story, questions were asked. Questions Charles didn't have the answers to, but Raina did. Charles wanted these answers from her in private but recognized too much time had passed, and they must be shared with everybody. Answers he hoped that would shed light on Maxwell's behavior. Also, he wished they could help to bring the end to Shears's reign of terror.

Chapter Twenty

"**WHAT I DO NOT** understand is why Maxwell has aligned himself with Shears?" Ivy said.

"It was his mission by instruction from the Crown." Raina answered.

"What was his full mission?" Thorn asked.

"I do not have knowledge on the full extent of his mission. All I was privy to was that he needed to present Shears with the jewels for information."

"What information?" asked Charles.

Raina sighed. She realized this time would come. Her time was over. She would have to explain her part in this mad scheme.

"Information on the whereabouts of the King's bastard."

The room grew quiet at this bit of information. Everybody in England was aware of the numerous affairs the King indulged himself in, but nobody had knowledge of any children out of wedlock he might have sired.

"I take it Shears has information about this child."

"Not only does he have information, he is holding the child hostage."

If the bedroom could grow any quieter from a few seconds ago, it did now. They all were acquainted with the horrors of Shears, especially how he treated women and children. An understanding filled the air.

"Maxwell is to give Shears the jewels, and then Shears has promised he would take him to the child. Only, Maxwell has no jewels to give to Shears."

"Where are they?"

"I have lost them. I hid them in a jewelry box, but I seem to have misplaced the trinket and the jewels."

"I have your jewelry box. I've kept it since the tavern, when you were disguised as a pregnant wench. But I saw none of these so-called jewels inside the box."

"You stole my jewelry box?"

"I didn't think someone as lowly as you should own something so exquisite. I thought you stole it, so I was going to find its rightful owner."

"You had no right to steal my possession. My parents gave me the gift. it was the only thing I had left of them."

"I am sorry for my mistake. If Thorn will send Sims to the room I stayed in before we left, he will find in among my things."

Raina did not respond to his apology. She realized it was a common mistake. She was portraying an untrustworthy character at the time. But in the time they spent together, he should have discussed this with her. But instead he kept this information to himself. It seemed like he still did not trust her.

Charles realized he was wrong in stealing her property and not returning it to her, even after they had come together. It was a sign of mistrust. In truth, he had forgotten about it until she had spoken of it just then. From the looks of things, she was furious with him. It would take a lot of honesty between them before they could trust one another.

"This explains why Maxwell is acting as he is, but it does not explain your involvement with Shears at the time of Charles's kidnapping," Thorn stated.

"I was recruited by Shears after I escaped your ship all those years ago. In my misguided anger toward you, I worked alongside him to destroy you. After I found out about his involvement with my family's death, I vowed to ruin him. I went to your government and gave them the information they needed to bring Shears to justice. So as a result, I continue to work for them. To gradually destroy Shears's entire operation, one warehouse at a time until they are all destroyed."

"You split sides easily in this time of war. How are we supposed to trust that you are working on our side and not have been pretending to help Shears?" Thorn asked.

"I understand why you would question my trust. But see this from the perspective of someone who has lost everybody they love from evil. I will do everything in my power to bring him down. You can either learn to trust me and work with me, or I will leave this house tonight and you will never hear from me again."

"If she leaves, then so do I," Charles seconded.

"Nobody is leaving here tonight. We are a family, and we will work together to rid ourselves of this evil. I am including you in this family, Raina. We are your family now. Is this understood?" The duke said, looking around at everybody. They all gave him a nod of understanding.

"Good, now that is settled. What is the plan now?" the duke asked.

"We wait for Maxwell," Thorn answered.

"Why would Maxwell come here?" asked Charles.

"For the jewels," answered Raina.

"Why don't we send a messenger to him with the jewels Raina has?" Ivy asked.

"Because my jewels are not the only ones he needs," Raina answered while looking in Thorn's direction.

All eyes turned toward him, but Thornhill never flinched. He sat there looking as arrogant as ever. He recognized he held a piece to Maxwell's dilemma, and he did not care. The gentleman who was once a friend had betrayed him and his family. All for what? He realized Raina knew more than she was letting everybody know, but he believed what she knew was not pertinent enough to hear about. The information would be between her and Charles to discuss and come to an understanding over. He noticed their relationship had developed and grown stronger while they were away. It was not his place to interfere. Charles believed himself in love with her. While he could see the signs were mutual, he still didn't trust the lady. She had knifed him, kidnapped Charles, disappeared, and her exploits were questionable on whose side she was fighting for. While she was coming clean with them, he still withheld his judgment on her until her actions proved otherwise. For his wife's sake, he would keep an open mind.

Thorn acknowledged her words with a nod of his head., "It is true I hold the one jewel he desires. He had it in his possession at one time but lost it as he freed Shears on the beach during the night we rescued you. Maxwell has yet to return for it."

"He will come for it," Raina said.

"And when he does, I will be waiting for him," Thorn threatened.

"That will solve nothing. He must have the ruby to finish his mission."

"As long as Maxwell is involved with Shears, I won't let him have possession of the jewel."

"You are standing in the way of the Crown's mission."

"I am saving many innocent lives."

"Do you think holding onto the ruby will prevent Shears from his vengeance?"

"No, but it will slow his progress. As long as his progress is slowed, then we have a chance of ending him."

"You are a fool, Thornhill," Raina ranted. "You are only giving him ammunition. There is a greater force than Shears at play here. Many influential men support him here in London. You need to bring them to justice along with Shears if you want to end this battle."

"Then ending their terror is precisely what we will do."

"How do you propose we do that?" asked Charles.

He had stayed silent while Raina and Thorn battled out their indifferences. There were still a lot of trust issues between them. He understood both of their reasoning and was caught in the middle. While he wanted to defend the woman he loved, he also wanted the same answers Thorn was demanding from her. So, in silence he gathered the information he heard and understood Raina that had been hurt deeply and was only trying to protect her heart. She wanted to trust them but didn't know how. It was up to him and the rest of his family to show her.

Sliding his hand over, he held her hand. It was an action to show her and his family he fully supported and trusted her. He felt her hesitation at his touch in front of his family, but her body relaxed, and her hand tightened in his. Looking up from their joined hands, he caught the stares from his family one by one. First his eyes met Ivy's, and she smiled her support and encouragement. He could always count on her to back him up. Next, he met his father's smile—one of approval. Then his eyes encountered Thorn's.

The message that passed between them was one of questioning then turned to acceptance. With his family's support, he knew all would be well.

"I will lure Maxwell to us. If what you are saying is true, I think we can talk sense into him."

"How will you do that?" asked Ivy.

Thorn turned his head to her. "I am afraid we will have to use you as bait, my dear."

That brought a huge smile to Ivy's face. She was becoming frustrated at being treated like an invalid in her particular state. She was pregnant, true, but she was not without means. This would be a way for her to show her friend's innocence. She understood their hesitance to trust Zane, but she experienced another side of him they did not. She knew she could convince him of their help.

"Do not look so frightened, my dear sister," Charles said sarcastically.

"I realize every one of you are angry with him, and I understand. He has disappointed me too. But he needs our help now more than ever," explained Ivy.

"Always the optimist. You remind me of your mother. She always championed the misunderstood," reminisced the duke.

Thorn sighed. "I am only using you as an enticement. You will have no contact with him."

"Whatever you say, darling." Ivy smiled at Thorn, expressing her devotion.

Everybody in the suite noticed it to be what it was. It was the look of obedience, but everyone knew Ivy did not have one iota of obedience in her body. She only placated Thorn with her words. They knew there would be action later that they would not have control of. Once Maxwell was drawn into the trap, Ivy would involve herself too. All they could do was to prevent it from happening.

It was decided that they would lure Maxwell into a trap at Hillston House with the rumor of Ivy's grief at the demise of her brother, causing her to be near death. It should keep the ton from visiting as well. Nobody wanted to go near the sickbed. This would the busybodies from discovering that Charles was alive. Then the rumors could circulate, Shears would think he succeeded, and Maxwell could complete part of his mission. They would draw him in with Ivy's sickness. They felt he could not stay away from his devoted friend. When he appeared, they would sit him down and come to some kind of reasoning with him. If their plan failed, there was nothing else they could do for Maxwell. He would fall in with Shears and the many others who were betraying the Crown.

Chapter Twenty-One

IVY WAS TIRED OF pretending to be on her deathbed. She snuck to the library to grab a book after Thorn had departed for the day. Most of the servants were sent away on holiday. They thought the fewer people who knew of Ivy's health, and Charles and Raina's presence, the better. Only the most trusted servants stayed in residence. The family had hired them years ago and knew they would not betray them. So, with few servants to wonder of her whereabouts, Ivy went in search of some reading material to pass the time. Also, she needed the exercise; while she longed for the garden, she knew it was not possible to risk being seen. So, she wandered the halls. The baby had taken up a continuous kick to register his or her objection to their relaxation the last few days.

As she passed Thorn's study, she heard a whisper of a noise. It sounded of drawers being slowly opened and shut. She knew Thorn had left; she watched as his carriage pulled away. It was not Charles or Raina either, because they had disguised themselves as servants and left to search for Maxwell undetected. She was alone in the house except for the servants. When she pushed the door open, she saw him.

His dark head was bent as he searched the drawers to Thorn's desk. He had lost weight, and his clothes were in disarray. This was not the gentleman who had kissed her in a closet months earlier. No, this was a desperate man.

Sliding inside the room, she turned the lock on the door as she closed it. She'd wanted to close it quietly, the lock slid into place with a clunk. A loud clunk. The man stilled. Then he gradually slid the drawer closed before he raised his head. When his eyes met hers, they held a haunted expression. She couldn't place the look exactly, but she realized it was not a joyful emotion.

"You don't appear to be on your last breath."

"No."

He laughed. Sweeping his hair back from his face, he continued laughing as he slipped into Thorn's chair. Once he finished laughing, he smiled at her with the charming grin he used on every lady to get what he wanted. While Ivy had always been immune to his charms, she still enjoyed the pleasure of his smiles. The haunted gaze disappeared from his eyes. While they still held a glimpse of what Ivy could not explain, they were not as dark.

"You were the pawn in their trick."

Ivy blushed at his harsh words. "Yes," she replied.

"Should have known, but the thought of you suffering brought me to my knees. I never meant to cause you any pain."

"You must not be suffering much, considering you are rifling through Thorn's desk."

"Your husband has an object of mine in his possession."

"I know."

"Of course you do. So, when is Thorn going to stage his entrance? Or are you supposed to lure me to him?"

"It is not as dramatic as you are making it out to be, Zane."

Zane raised his eyebrow in question in the maddening way he always did when somebody tried to prove him wrong. "Isn't it?" he questioned.

Ivy sighed. "No."

He humphed but rose from the desk and made his way to her side. Maxwell slid his arm around her as he helped her to the settee to sit. Then he made his way over to the bookshelves. Pulling several books out, he continued in his search. He was sure Thorn hid the ruby in this room. When he moved a book slightly forward, he heard the soft click. He smiled as he brought the volume farther out, releasing the special compartment. He blocked Ivy's view from what he was doing. Slipping his hand inside, he wrapped his fingers around his prize. He rubbed the smooth surface of the jewel. Maxwell pulled it out and slid the book back in place. He palmed the ruby in his hand as he turned toward Ivy. When he faced her again, he noticed she was trying to move her body to see his actions. Sliding his hands inside his pockets, he moved from the shelves and wandered around the room, overturning items as he moved.

"Have you located what you are searching for?"

"You know I have not," he said as casually to her as he could.

Sitting next to Ivy, he regarded her. With his eyes half closed, he took in the picture of her absolute charm. Even heavy with child she was as lovely as ever. Her long, blonde hair was loose and flowing around her shoulders. She positively glowed. Thorn was a lucky bastard.

"I see Thornhill is taking excellent care of you."

"You knew he would."

"At one time I wondered, but I can see the fool followed through in the end."

"Mm, yes." Ivy responded as she rubbed her belly.

"I guess my chances are over?" he teased.

Ivy laughed, "You had zero chances to begin with."

"Ah, but a man can wonder."

Ivy laughed at his wry sense of humor. Only Zane could make an uncomfortable scene comfortable. But she could see he wasn't the same. She wanted to help him while she could before the others arrived. Her part of the plan was to keep him occupied for as long as possible. She could do that. Spending time with Zane had never been a hardship. If it were not for him, loneliness would have been her companion while Thorn was away fighting in the war. But it was Zane who befriended her when she needed him the most. Now it was her turn to be there for him.

"Is it her?"

"Yes, I believe so."

"Will you let Thorn and Charles help you?"

"No, I will not have their lives on my conscience too."

"How are you going to rescue her?"

"That is a plan I am trying to figure out."

"If you rescue her, what will become of her?"

"What should have been offered to her ages ago."

"It was not your fault, Zane. You were but a child yourself."

"That is where you are wrong, Ivy. I was old enough to recognize what they were doing was wrong. I could've prevented all of this from happening."

Ivy laid her hand on his arm. "You know this is wrong. You did not have the power to stop them. Cease blaming yourself."

"Maybe, but I have the power now. The power to bring her home and right all the wrongs."

"Please let me tell Thorn your story. We can help you."

"Ivy, you made me a promise years ago, and I am holding you to it. Please do not betray my trust in this matter. I realize that is a lot for me to ask of you, considering how I have betrayed you countless times in the past year, but this secret is sacred. Nobody knows of your knowledge on this matter. If you make this known to Thorn and the others, you are putting everybody's lives at risk." As he laid his hand on her rounded stomach, feeling the life stirring beneath his fingertips. "I will not have you risk your happiness for my sorry soul. Will you continue to offer me your secrecy in this matter?"

"I promise," Ivy whispered.

"Now that everything is settled, I have brought Thorn and you a wedding present. I want to offer my humblest apologies for not attending your nuptials. By bringing a present with me, I hope you can find it in your hearts to forgive me."

"I adore presents. Where is it?"

Maxwell rose from the sofa and sauntered over to the window. Hidden behind the curtains was a package wrapped gaily in pastel paper. Making his way back to her side, he saw her excitement. She was practically bouncing up and down. Ivy always loved to be spoiled. He hoped this would help repair a few of his wrongdoings where she was concerned. He handed her the present and stood back as she ripped the paper away.

"Oh," she exclaimed, tears filling her eyes.

Her fingers lightly reached out to touch the hand-crafted picture frame. She dipped her fingers along the curve in the border. Looking up at him, she smiled through the tears sliding along her cheeks.

"Thank you so much, Zane. This is the most wonderful present I have ever received. I know precisely where we will hang it."

Zane smiled at her enjoyment. He recognized the tears to be ones of joy.

"Do you remember when I sketched this?"

Ivy smiled at the memory. "Yes. I was so down in the dumps, and you helped me that day not to give up hope."

"It all worked out for you. You are happy, are you not, Ivy?"

"Yes, it all worked out, and I am very happy."

Zane nodded. "Then I am happy for you."

They were both quiet, neither one of them wanting to break their repaired friendship. Their bond was still fragile from the lies and deception, but both understood it was a friendship that would stand the test of time.

"I must be off, my dear. Please give my regards to Thorn."

"Please stay, Zane. I beg of you."

"I realize keeping me here is your mission, but I must run."

"But you didn't find what you came to Hillston House for."

"Ah, but I did. I came to pay my respects to your family for your loss and to see to my dear friend's welfare. I think I have achieved what I have set out to do. Please give Thorn and your family my regards."

He lifted her hand and bestowed a kiss across her knuckles. As he made his way to the door, he departed the same way he entered. Walking through the door, he continued to the servant's entrance and swiftly exited through the back garden.

Ivy tried to rise from the settee and follow him, but her cumbersome body stopped her from his quick departure. She had only made it as far as the door when Thorn came rushing into his study.

"Where is he?"

"He left."

"Damn."

"Thorn."

"Sorry, my dear. I was so close to capturing him."

"I tried."

"That you did my dear." Thorn helped her to sit back on the sofa.

Lowering himself next to her, he brought her into the circle of his arms. Leaning them both back against the settee he sighed. When Sims had sent word that Ivy was with Maxwell in the study, he knew their plan had worked. He rushed home to rescue her, but he was too late.

"Zane brought us a wedding present."

"Did he now?"

"Yes, a painting. I think we will hang the portrait in our bedroom."

"Wherever you wish, my love."

"Will you look at it?"

"I am sure I will love the picture if you do."

"Please look."

Thorn sighed, releasing his arms from around Ivy. He sat forward and lifted the image to the light. When he saw what the painting was, he laughed. The last time he had looked upon this picture, it had put him in a jealous rage. But after he heard the story behind the picture, he found a new sense of friendship toward Maxwell and a love forever binding him with Ivy.

It was a picture of his beloved Ivy sitting near the lake, giggling at ducks waddling by, with a look of enchanted love written all over her face. At first, he believed the picture meant Ivy in love with the artist, but it really reflected the love she felt for him. His friend had made her remember him and their love for each other. This picture was an act of forgiveness. He laughed at the humor of the present. Maxwell was still Maxwell. Nothing had changed with the man.

He looked over at Ivy. "I agree that the bedroom will make a lovely home for this masterpiece. One day, we will remember and laugh over this memory."

"He refused."

"I understand why, and you are correct in your assumption of the man. I now see that while he is misguided, he is doing what a true friend would do for the safety of those he loves."

"Are we still going to help him?"

"Yes, my dear, we are." He pulled Ivy back into his arms and gently kissed her with small light kisses that made them whole. Sitting back, they admired their wedding present from their friend.

~~~~~~

It had been a week, and they had spent most of their time apart—in more ways than one. When they had spent time together, it was in the presence of others. The duke had insisted Charles return to their townhome and Raina stay with the Thornhills for propriety's sake. Which was preposterous, considering that the last few weeks they were alone at the cottage. She missed him. But what made it even worse was that he had not spoken to her about her confessions, which made her believe he was angry with her deception.

But they were alone together now. They waited in disguise across the back lane for any signs of Maxwell. Both were dressed in servant clothes. They waited in silence, stuck behind several tall hedges. The silence was killing her, but she was too afraid to speak for what he might say to her. Over the course of the last few days, she realized the true depths of her feelings for him. She loved him deeply. Raina wanted a life with him after they destroyed Shears. Her only doubt was if he cared the same way for her anymore. She knew he did at the cottage, but much had changed since then. Did his feelings change too? She needed to quit being such a coward and ask him, but she didn't. She stayed next to his side and kept her thoughts to herself.

Finally, they were alone. And what did he do but stand in silence like an idiot. An idiot so in love with her he wanted to confess it, but he knew this was not the place. He wanted to woo her in a romantic setting when he professed his love and asked for her hand in marriage. She deserved romance, especially after what she had endured the past few years. He wanted to make her feel cherished. But they needed to bring Shears and his cohorts to justice first. In time, he would profess his love and propose to her.

He'd reflected upon their relationship during their time apart. He listened as she told of her acts of desperation. She was a lady abandoned, who did what she did to survive. He knew she regretted her acts of revenge. Well, some of them anyhow. She regretted kidnapping him and stabbing Thorn, but not Shears's eventual destruction. He could not blame her there. While many of her plans were somewhat misguided, they were done with the best intent. What troubled him was how reckless she was with her own life. He understood that she believed she had nothing to live for, but did she still feel that way? He hoped not. He hoped she wanted the same things he did.

"We will marry," he blurted out abruptly.

Where had that come from? Now he sounded like a pompous jackass. *Real romantic there, Mallory. Way to sweep her off her feet.* He wanted to smack himself upside the head. What happened to waiting for a romantic atmosphere?

Well, so much for expecting a romantic gesture from Charles. Now he feels obligated to marry me. Raina could view his offer one of two ways. One, he felt he had to marry her, and they could try to build a life together, rebuild the trust between them, and learn to love each other. Or two, they marry out of necessity and live separate lives. Not that she wanted number two. But if she agreed, she could make number one become a reality. For so long, she lived her life in a haze, her anger dictating her actions. She now had the opportunity to live her life fully. Did it matter how she was asked or in this case, demanded?

She never turned toward him but continued staring out across Thornhills' garden when she answered him. "All right."

All right, as in yes? That was all she said. No arguments, only a meek "all right." This was not his Raina. He let out a lengthy sigh of relief. He would take this affirmative answer as a positive sign, even though it didn't speak to her personality to be so agreeable. But before he questioned her farther, their prey strolled out of the garden as casually as a wanted chap could be.

Raina noticed him first. While the distraction of the awkward proposal was still featured on her mind, she had never taken her eyes off the garden. Granted it was looking there or looking at Charles's reaction to her acceptance. She watched as Maxwell lazily strolled out of the garden and walked along the hedges they were hidden behind.

"You two must work on your disguises. I spotted you the minute I entered the residence. You are slipping, poor girl. Must be the love that sparkles between you two that makes you so vulnerable," Maxwell quipped.

Before they could reply to him, he spoke to the groomsman nearby, requesting his horse be brought to him. Charles and Raina both realized they were too caught up in their own minds to have noticed that he had stabled his horse and gained entry to the house. They had failed Ivy and themselves. When the groomsman brought the horse to Maxwell, he made a fuss with the cinches on the saddle and was pretending to speak to the horse.

"I am being watched, along with the house. Don't come from behind the hedges to confront me. The rumor of your deaths has spread, and Shears believes it's true. Do not show your faces, or it will ruin everything I have set to achieve."

"But you need every jewel for your plan to work," Charles hissed through the hedges.

Maxwell patted his pocket, smiling smugly. "What makes you think I do not have every one of them?"

"Because Raina has the small jewels in her jewelry box, and Thorn has hidden the one you need the most."

"Tsk, tsk. Raina, dear, you still aren't being honest with him, are you? This won't work for your marriage, all this dishonesty. Shall you tell him, or shall I?"

"Charles…" Raina began hesitantly.

"We don't have time for this. I must leave. Let me make this quick for you, Mallory. Raina gave me the jewels two nights ago. As for the main jewel, there is not a hiding space I cannot find. Good day to you both."

With that, Maxwell climbed upon his horse and trotted away. Which left Raina stuck behind the hedges with Charles. She could see the anger radiating off him. She knew it would make Charles angry when she met with Maxwell to give him the jewels, but while she loved and respected Charles, she still had to complete her mission for the Crown. And the mission was to help Maxwell retrieve the jewels and the missing heir. Or else it was her life. This was one bit of information she had not shared with them. Her very life hung in the balance. There would be no way they could stop the Crown from having her killed. It was a higher power they had no influence over. For her aid in helping Maxwell, the Crown would wave away every accusation against her for Charles's kidnapping. If she did not complete the mission, her death would suffice.

The silence, while unbearable before, was threating to choke her now. In response to Maxwell's words, Charles wrapped his hand around her arm, tightening his hold. His anger was clear. As he dragged her toward the stables, he spoke not a word. He ordered the groomsman to escort her safely to the house as he stomped to his horse's stall.

"Charles, let me explain."

He held up his hand for her silence. "Not now, Raina. I am not in the mood for any more of your lies. Please see to Ivy's safety. I will return shortly."

"But—"

"What a fool I have been, concerning myself over your welfare. Still you have no faith in me to protect you. Your opinion of me must be very insignificant."

"No, that is not the case. It is not what you think. Maxwell twisted my involvement with him to distract you."

"Is what he said true?"

"Yes."

"That is all I need to hear. Now please see to Ivy for me."

With those last words, he left the stable for an unknown destination. While Raina doubted he would return, she only hoped he was aware of his surroundings and stayed safe. She followed the groomsman back to the house and went in search of Ivy. She found her in Thorn's study. Ivy was wrapped in Thorn's arms in an intimate moment. Raina backed out of the room and made her way upstairs not wanting to disturb them. Ivy was safe, not that she was in any danger to begin with. From what she knew of Maxwell, he would never harm his friend. Not Ivy. Not any of them. Ivy had faith in Maxwell. If only everybody else could too.

Chapter Twenty-Two

CHARLES SLAMMED THE DOOR TO HIS father's townhome in anger. How could she continue to keep lying to them? Especially him. Discarding himself of his disguise, he stormed into his father's study and poured himself a scotch. His drink of choice. While others preferred the malt flavor of whiskey, he preferred the smoother taste of scotch. But one was not enough. After his third drink, he took the decanter with him. Sliding into the overstuffed brown leather chair by the fire, he drank his anger, fear, and love away.

Why did she risk her life and not confide in him? Still after everything they had been through, she continued to lie to him. And the fool that he was, he put the offer of marriage on the table to her. How she must have been laughing to herself before she so readily agreed. Of course marriage to him would be a better alternative than to wherever else her life was leading her to. Yes, she tried to explain to him. Explain what? More lies on top of the ones she previously spoke? Then there was the fact that she continued putting his family's lives at risk with her actions. Why did she continue to aid Maxwell? Particularly when she sowed the seeds of doubt about his character. Or was this another ploy to draw attention from her? Charles didn't know what to have faith in now. He wanted to believe in the love he felt for her, but she was causing him to doubt her too much.

This is where Thorn and his father found him a few hours later, too soused from drink to make any sense. He mumbled his feelings of love for her and her lies to them. As they fed him cups of coffee, one after the other, he saw the looks of pity on their faces—and looks of compassion filled with humor.

"Bugger off, both of you."

"Is that how you speak to your father?"

"No, sir," he humbly replied.

But it only earned him more laughter. They were laughing at him. Did they not understand the severity of the situation? They were harboring a treasonous wench.

"Well I would not refer to your future wife as a wench in her company, my son."

"Or in the company of others," Thorn drawled.

Did he actually speak his last thought aloud? He must have for their comments. What a fool he was.

"Love usually does that to a man."

Again, he was speaking what he should keep to himself. Oh well, he might as well tell them of her deception. They could decide how to handle her. He no longer wanted her on his hands.

"We already know. She told us what happened with Maxwell today and told us the full truth," Thorn explained.

"You will wed her this evening. I have a special license from the Archbishop himself. You will offer her your protection. After the wedding, it will be for you to decide how you want the marriage to proceed. But my advice to you is to hear her out and do not turn your back on this rare gift of love. It only happens once in a lifetime. Do not let your pride stand in the way," his father told him.

"But she is still lying to us. Raina is looking out for herself and doesn't care for the lives of others."

"You would too if your own life hung in the balance."

"What are you talking about?"

"The Crown told her to complete the mission or forfeit her life," Thorn said.

"Explain yourself," demanded Charles.

"After we found you on the beach and Shears escaped, we reported the incident to the Crown. They seized the weapons and his men. They declared that anybody who aided Shears would find themselves hung without a trial. Raina's name was the first on the list. She had kidnapped you and held you against your will for Shears. For that, she was guilty. When she went to them with a plan to destroy Shears, she was presented with the charges for her execution. She was told if she complied with their plans, they would dismiss all charges. If not, then Raina would hang. So, she worked undercover with Maxwell on retrieving the jewels and destroying Shears."

"How was she supposed to do this?"

"Shears's payment to the people who aided him was in the jewels. Raina infiltrated every town along the way and stole the payments. After she stole the jewels, she destroyed the shipments of illegal guns in Shears's warehouses along the coast."

"Why did she place herself at risk?"

"I think you already know the answer to your question, son."

Charles processed this new information and understood the severity of her actions.

"She wanted to atone for her past deeds."

"And?" Thorn prompted.

"She loves me."

"I think he is finally getting it, George."

"Yes, I see that he is."

"Then why didn't she confess her mission to begin with?"

"Her mission is not complete. Until it is, she will not be free from the Crown."

"What does she have left to do? She gave Maxwell the jewels."

"Yes, and he found the other one in my study this afternoon."

"Then what?"

"Until Maxwell has the information he seeks and completes his mission, Raina will always be in danger. It is up to us to help Maxwell succeed to be able to free Raina."

"That is why you will marry her tonight, so we can protect her better," ordered his father.

"No, I will marry her tonight because I love her. I am such a fool. I should have listened to her. She wanted to explain, but I walked away from her."

"Well, only you can make this right. You need to get yourself upstairs and clean your drunken mess. Tonight, I get myself another daughter. It has been a long time coming. Now go, you don't want to be late for your own wedding."

Charles pulled himself off the chair with a huge grin. It was all going to end well. He may be a fool, but he was a fool in love. Before they wed, he would profess his love and tell her of his trust in her and that he would never doubt her again.

~~~~~~

Raina sat before the mirror as Mabel dressed her hair. Red beads were interwoven between her dark tresses. The duke had a gown sent over for her to wear for her wedding. The dress included a letter that explained how he would be honored for his new daughter to wear the gown. Ivy had explained that it had been her mama's. When asked if it bothered her that she was to wear it when Ivy herself didn't for her own wedding, Ivy laughed in response. She replied she was too short to wear the dress, and Raina was of the height and the stature of her mother. She was delighted Papa had sent the gown for her. Feeling better, Raina allowed them to dress her in the elegant white creation. There were lace and pearls adorning the train, while the upper half of the dress was covered in silk. Smooth to the touch. Tiny buttons adorned the back of the dress. Once Mabel was done with her hair, Ivy dismissed the maid.

As she stood up, Raina turned in a full circle, asking Ivy how she looked.

Ivy smiled her appreciation. "Gorgeous. You will knock my brother for a loop."

"I feel your brother will not notice me through his anger."

"Nonsense. By now, Thorn and Father will have talked a bit of sense into him."

"By which you mean they will have forced him here to wed me."

Laughing, Ivy responded, "Believe me, there will be no force tonight. Trust me when I say you will only see the love in his eyes when you say your vows to one another."

"I want to believe this, but you weren't present today when he left. He would not even look at me, and I could feel his anger in my gut."

"That was then. This is now."

Raina listened to Ivy, but she did not believe her. She heard a carriage below and went to the window. She pulled back the curtain and saw Charles alight from his father's carriage. Following him was the duke and Thorn. They were laughing and appeared to be in good spirits. As Charles looked up, he caught sight of her watching him. He waved the men ahead as he continued to watch her. Their gaze did not part from one another, speaking the unspoken words their hearts could not tell each other. Touching her fingers to the glass, her answer was a small nod. Then he disappeared up the front steps. Raina sighed as she pulled back. She thought his eyes were telling her of his forgiveness and his love, but his nod and disappearance spoke of something else entirely.

A knock upon the door turned her around as Ivy answered. A servant handed Ivy a jewelry case with instructions for Raina.

Ivy smiled as she handed Raina the note and case. "Maybe this will put your mind at ease."

Raina opened the letter:

My darling Raina,

I hope you will forgive a fool for his actions and wear this gift to you as a token of my love.

This necklace belonged to my mother. I have worn it around my neck since she died as a remembrance to her. I gave it to you once to wear to save my life, and you did. Today, I am giving it to you again to wear, but this time I would like for you to wear it for the love we share with one another.

Please adorn yourself with my gift and love.

I wait below anxiously for your hand in marriage.

Your devoted servant and soon to be husband. Also, the man who loves you with his life.

Charles

Raina opened the case. It was the ruby necklace she had worn months earlier to Ivy and Thorn's betrothal ball. She wore it for Ivy to find her. It was the evening she had sacrificed her own goals for those of another. With shaking fingers, she touched the jewel. Raina lifted the necklace and fastened it around her neck. Her fingers kept tracing the jewel as she reread the letter.

He wanted to marry her. He loved her. Smiling, she looked up and saw the other woman returning her smile of joy.

"Mama's dress and necklace. Her memory will be strong tonight. See, I told you. Now we shall be sisters, but not if we do not get you downstairs."

"He loves me, doesn't he?" Raina asked in awe.

"Yes, my dear."

Raina could not wait to see him. All would be well in time. Now she knew all she needed to do was to have faith in their love and it would guide them along the way. She rushed toward the door and opened it. Charles stood there in hesitation, but Raina did not give him any time to wonder. She launched herself in his arms and pulled his head down for a kiss. It was no chaste kiss. It was a kiss of undying love. The kind of kiss that says what words could never describe. She poured her love into the kiss with one slow touch at a time.

Charles had been scared to knock. Afraid of her reaction to their quick, impromptu wedding, but when she appeared in the doorway and threw herself in his arms, he had his answer. At least what he was hoping for, anyhow. Her kiss upon his lips poured out her love for him, so in return, he spoke of his. Their lips entwined with their passion as each stroke of the tongue drove their love deeper. When he pulled back from the kiss, he rested his forehead against hers and stared into her eyes.

"I love you," he whispered.

"I love you," she whispered back.

Three simple words spoken to each other. The words made everything click into place and doused their fears and doubts into oblivion. Simple words that needed no more explanation.

"Now that is all settled, are we having a wedding this evening or not?" Ivy quipped from behind them.

Charles turned with Raina pressed tightly next to his side. "Yes, my dear sister, I believe we are."

"Then go below, brother. We will be along shortly." She tried to shush him away with her hands.

"No, I am not letting her out of my sight again."

Ivy laughed. "Very well."

They could hear her laughter echoing from the staircase as she made her way below.

"Charles?"

Placing a soft kiss on her lips, he said, "Shh, we will talk later. I was a fool before. Let us rejoice in this happy occasion. There will be time for explanations later."

She sighed. It would have to do. She was confident and secure in their love now to know they could solve all their problems. Tonight was her wedding night, an evening she used to dream about when she was younger but dismissed over the years after tragedy had taken over her life. It was a time for rejoicing. Raina had a chance at a new beginning, one which would be filled with love, the love she had seen between her father and mother when she was young.

Turning back, she ran back into her room and retrieved jewelry box he had returned to her. Raina pulled out the worn blue handkerchief and wrapped it around the flowers Ivy had arranged for her to hold during the wedding ceremony. His mother's dress and necklace, his love, now a piece of love from her parents. The token made this complete.

Charles fingered the material. "Your father's?"

"Yes, Mama made it for him for their wedding day."

Charles smiled endearingly at her small gesture. "A fine addition for our wedding. Now all who we love and miss will be remembered on our special day."

He offered his arm to her, and they made their way downstairs, where his father, Thorn, and Ivy awaited them. Ivy had decorated the library with roses from her garden, and candlelight bounced off the walls, creating a warm glow in the room. Charles walked her in front of a man of the cloth, who married them.

When asked who gave the bride away, every occupant in the room gave their approval. It was a sign to Raina as her acceptance into their family, a sign of forgiveness from Thorn, and love from her new family. She would give none of them doubt again for their tokens of love.

When he announced them husband and wife, Charles swept her into a passionate kiss, which held promises of what was to come later when they were alone. The preacher had to cough his disapproval many times before Charles released her lips.

After the kiss, hugs were given to the wedded couple. Ivy then directed them to the dining room for a celebration dinner and wedding cake. As they dined and celebrated the wedding, Charles and Raina could not help to laugh and share a private joke as the wedding cake was served. They thought of the last time they had their wedding cake. This wasn't their first wedding cake, but it would be their last.

Chapter Twenty-Three

THEY STOOD BEFORE THE glow of the fireplace. A few inches separated them, each staring into each other's eyes. The room was lit with candles, with rose petals decorating the floor and bed. Ivy had worked her magic while they wed. A bottle of wine sat chilled near the window, with a spread under a tray for them to enjoy later.

Neither of them moved. The air sparkled with their passion for one another, savoring the moment of being alone at last. Charles lifted his hands and pulled out the jeweled pins from her hair, watching as it draped over his hands, her long black tresses curling around his fingers. He slid his fingers through her glorious mane, luxuriating in the touch of its softness. She still did not move, but she watched him with heavy, leaden eyes. When he ran his thumb across her lips, she moaned and closed her eyes. Her eyelashes fluttered across her cheeks. When he spread her lips open with his thumb, she opened her eyes, her tongue slowly darting between her lips to sample him. A flick of her tongue against his thumb brought his other hand to her head, drawing her to his lips.

His lips devoured her, his tongue drew her lips open farther, sliding in to savor her. She tasted of honey, sweet honey. A flavor he hungered for and craved more of. When her tongue joined his, he was undone. His desire for her grew into a reckless passion. Not one kiss or touch was enough. He was starved for her.

Raina sensed the strength of his passion from the first touch of his hands on her hair. His eyes told her of his desire for her, but nothing compared to the touch and taste of him. She needed to be with him, to have his body join hers. As she slid her hand through his thick hair, she pulled him closer to her body. Pressing her hips against his, her breasts against his chest, she understood his need for her. She gently pressed her hips against his again, and he moaned and pressed his hardness into her. Raina wanted to feel his body against hers, so she started to unbutton his clothes.

Charles pulled back from their kiss and took a deep breath. This was moving too fast. He wanted to savor her all night. Nice and slow. Every kiss, every touch lasting forever. He laughed at her moan of impatience. She was as eager as he was.

He pulled her hands into his and kissed each palm, his lips tracing a path to her wrists, then to the bend in her elbow and back again. When he stared into her eyes, he saw everything. Love. Desire. Need. Want. Passion.

"I want to take this slow tonight."

Her only answer was a moan. He chuckled. After he turned her around, he twisted her hair to drape down the front of her dress. Kissing the back of her neck, his lips made their way to the buttons of her dress. He unhooked each button, his fingers leaving a trail along her back as the dress spread open wider.

"You look exquisite in this dress. A vision in white. I have been aching for you the entire evening," he whispered in her ear.

Another moan.

With her buttons unhooked, he swept the dress off her body. When he turned her back around, she stood before him in a red chemise. Her breasts were cupped with a thin piece of lace, her pink nipples peeking through. The chemise cupped her body tightly. White lace stockings graced her long legs, held together at her thighs with tiny rosebud clips. Now he was the one moaning. This would be torture, but he would give her a wedding night she would never forget.

Raina watched the effect she had on Charles and smiled. *Slow. We shall see.* While the idea of sweet romance for their wedding night was endearing, it would not be possible for either one of them. If his moan was any sign, her touch would ignite him. She knew she already was. His soft touches and kisses had her ready to explode.

"My turn, Lord Mallory," Raina told him as she untied his cravat. Slowly untying the knot, she moved closer to him so her breasts could rub against him. Her fingers next worked on the buttons of his vest and shirt. Once they came undone, she lifted the shirt over his head. Her nipples brushed across his bare chest. Now he was the one moaning.

Her fingers trailed across his chest, touching his scars and muscles as she went. Kneeling on the floor, she undid the buttons of his trousers. She slid open one button, and her hand brushed across his need for her. Her head was bent so he could not look at her tease of a smile. She gently placed a kiss on his hardness, so softly it felt like a soft whisper of wind. When her fingers slid along the length of his cock and wrapped around, slowly stroking, she realized the game was over when he bent and lifted her in his arms.

His mouth crushed hers in a passionate kiss as he carried her to the bed. Lowering her to the mattress, he swiftly followed. His lips devoured hers, their hands touching, sliding, caressing each other. Every single moan was kissed away and followed by more. There was no touch or kiss enough for either of them.

His hands stroked her breasts, while his lips brought her nipples to stiff peaks. While she writhed under his touch, hungry for more, he fed her hunger with more kisses. More touches. More passion until she begged for more. When he slid his finger into her wetness, stroking her passion higher, she cried out her need for him. But he wanted more from her, needed more from her. So, he continued to stroke her, his fingers sliding in and out of her as her body climbed higher and higher. When he noticed her body start to crest over, he slid inside her. Slowly. His body claimed hers as she had claimed his long ago. He felt her tighten around him. Her body clung to him as he gently stroked in and out of her hot wet heat.

Raina was clinging to Charles's body. Her body floated along as he made love to her. There were no words to describe how he made her feel, how he made her body come alive. Her fingers dug into his shoulders, wrapping her legs around him, and she moved her body with his, lost in each other as they became one.

Charles lowered his lips to hers and kissed her gently. Each pull of his lips against her was of softness. Gentle kisses as his body took her with him into a passionate eclipse. His fingers slid around her cheeks as he gazed into her eyes.

"I love you for eternity."

Tears leaked from her eyes as he spoke those words to her as their bodies exploded around each other. He kissed her tears away and pulled her close. As he wrapped his arms around her, he continued to whisper words of love to her as she cried in his arms. They were not tears of pain or regret. They were the tears of love, a love that made her complete.

~~~~~

Gradually coming awake in Charles's arms, she rolled over and pressed a kiss to his neck. He moaned and tightened his arms around her. Her lips continued a trail toward his.

"I love you too, Charles," she whispered.

His eyes opened at her words, and he pressed his mouth to her as softly as hers were to his. Soft and slow their lips entwined, tasting, and relishing in each other.

Raina sighed at the touch of his mouth against hers. When she pulled away, she rested her hands on his chest and watched him come more fully awake. He smiled affectionately at her, his fingers brushing the hair back from her face. They lay this way for a few moments, gently touching each other while stealing kisses.

Raina knew they needed to talk, but they needed this even more. This was a closeness they would share forever. To wake every morning in his arms would be a delight, as every evening would be a passion she could not wait to share with him. She realized he would always be there for her no matter what. Now all she had to do was to tell him the full truth of her involvement with Shears and Maxwell. She knew Thorn had told him of the Crown's threat to her life, but nobody knew of the full extent of her deception. It was time to share it with Charles.

Rolling out of the bed, she saw his shirt lying across a chair. She slid the shirt over her naked body and wandered over to the wine. When Raina lifted the lid, she saw a plate full of delicacies. She poured them both a drink and carried the plate over to the bed and offered them to Charles.

He eyed them skeptically. "Poisoning me again, my dear? I promise to make love to you longer next time."

Raina throatily laughed at his wry sense of humor. "Mm, I will take you up on that promise later. I swear everything is safe. This time, anyhow," she added with her own bit of humor.

That set Charles to laughing as he grabbed the plate and his wine glass. He set out to show her he believed her and ate the small sandwiches and sweets. If it was one thing she could take, it was the humor at her past misgivings toward him. He realized she needed to talk, but he wanted to make the atmosphere as light-hearted for her as he could. The topic was heavy, and they needed to move past it. But for that to happen, Raina needed to confess her lies to him. He reached out to pull her beside him and offered her a repast. As they dined, Raina told him of her involvement with Shears and what led her to working with Maxwell.

As she told her story, Charles never once interrupted her or condemned her actions. He showed his continued support by holding her hand and stroking her arm when she needed comfort. She started with the death of her mother and brother. Then she continued with her father's murder and how she believed Thorn had killed him. She swore revenge. She had known of Shears through her father and sought him out. Shears made her do inconceivable crimes against people to earn his trust. After she had earned his trust, she volunteered to kidnap Charles.

She had led Shears to Ivy and planted the seed in Shears's mind about absconding with Ivy. She had watched Maxwell undercover in London, and that is when she first learned of Ivy. As she infiltrated the ton, she heard of Ivy's love for Thornhill. Raina gave Shears this information and helped Shears concoct a plan to kill Charles and kidnap Ivy to draw Thornhill into their trap. By this time, Maxwell also worked for Shears, and Raina didn't trust him. But she could not express her doubts to Shears because she witnessed Maxwell doing things that left her in doubt of his true allegiance.

"After Ivy was kidnapped and you were left for dead, I finally saw how evil Shears was. I started to fear him. When nobody came to your rescue, I loaded you in a cart and drove to the cottage I had been renting. But you would not come around, and your health declined. More time passed, and I nursed you the best I could. Then I heard Maxwell sniffing around my place. He found me and saw the shape you were in. At that moment I knew the true line Maxwell was playing," Raina continued to explain.

"He cared too much for you and threatened to kill me. When I convinced him I was trying to save you and that I no longer was working for Shears, he helped me keep you safe. He told me of Ivy's kidnapping and how he knew the part I played. I had never felt guiltier. You see, I had come to care for you during that time. We talked; I know you do not remember. Most of the time you were incoherent, but you would talk about your family often. When Shears set out to kidnap Ivy again at her ball, we decided to stop him. I went to the ball, and that was where Thorn discovered me, but as awful as it was for me, it was a godsend for you. You were rescued and received the medical help you needed.

"But through all the deception, I realized the man I was working for was also the man who had my entire family murdered. I swore I would seek my revenge. In doing so, I contacted Maxwell, who put me in contact with the Crown. I pledged my life to destroy Shears. Since I was wanted for crimes against the Crown, they agreed to work with me if I could bring Shears to an end. In doing so, I set about bringing down Shears's operation. There wasn't a plan I wouldn't do. I stole, I lied, and I pretended to be many characters, doing everything to stop him.

"I am not proud of my behavior, but they were a means to an end. And I would do them over again to destroy him. But destroying Shears isn't enough for the Crown. They have a bigger agenda at hand. They need the jewels Maxwell has, and I was to help him get them. If he fails with his plan and does not complete his mission, then I am to kill him. He knows too much information. I had to help him succeed. I could not kill him, as he has helped me too much with destroying Shears. He has helped me find out information I needed, and he helped me destroy every building holding Shears's weapons. I cannot take his life, and I must help him achieve his goals. I know how he deceives you and your family, and I know I am asking an awful lot, but will you help me help him?"

Raina waited in silence for an answer from him. He had not spoken through her whole story. At times, she saw that he wanted to, but he held back. Not once did he let her hand go or cease touching her. The only behavior that changed was the look he bestowed on her. His eyes were expressive, changing from pity, to anger, to comfort, to fear, to pride. Through her whole story, they always held his love.

"I am sorry for the heartache I caused your family. I hope one day you will forgive me."

"There is nothing to forgive, Raina. I love you through all your faults, as I hope you will love me through mine. What you have endured over the course of time is amazing, as is the fact that you are still fighting strong. I am beyond proud of you."

"Will you help me?"

"Yes," he whispered as he pulled her in close to hold her.

They lay there holding each other as they thought of how if it were not for Shears they wouldn't be where they were today. How a villain constructed evil across all bounds but still played a hand in their relationship felt like parody.

As they whispered through the night of each other's unanswered questions, their words were interrupted often with touches and kisses. Each kiss becoming longer, where there were no words existed between each other. Just their passion. It was long into the evening when Raina whispered, "I think I will take you up on your promise now." Where in return Charles did. He loved her long into the night and through the next morning.

Chapter Twenty-Four

IT WASN'T UNTIL MIDAFTERNOON the next day before they made
their way downstairs. Holding hands and whispering secrets, they were two
young newlyweds in bliss. Sims directed them toward the parlor, where the
duke, Thorn, and Ivy awaited them. Charles sat Raina next to Ivy on the
divan, and he sat in a chair nearby.

"I trust you slept well last evening," the duke teased.

Charles muffled a chuckle after he saw his wife blush a delightful
shade of pink. In the entire time he had known her, he had never seen her
embarrassed. She had been subjected to a rougher crowd than his sister, so
he did not think such words could shock her, but they had. It would appear
his wife still held onto a bit of innocence after all. It was a refreshing
thought. He would have to see if the shade of pink traveled over the course
of the rest of her body. Of course, he would have to explore her reaction
another time. Charles decided to take pity upon his wife and poured her a
spot of tea, brushing a kiss across her cheek.

He whispered in her ear, "You are very becoming in pink, my dear."
Which only made her blush deepen.

She swatted him away while she busied herself with her tea. Adding
sugar and honey, she averted her eyes from them.

"Charles, leave her alone," Ivy said, taking pity on her new sister.

"Ignore them, Raina. You will get used to their teasing in time."

Raina smiled her appreciation at Ivy and inquired of her health. Ivy was near her time, and everybody showed concern for her well-being. She had not slowed any. Still involved in the day-to-day activities of running the townhome and taking care of Tommy, she never knew when to stop and rest. Thorn was forever following her, begging her to rest.

"What do we owe the pleasure of your company, Father?" Charles asked.

"My connections have sent word that Shears plans an attack tonight. It is time for us to move. I am afraid this time your wife will have to be the bait," Thorn informed them.

"Absolutely not," Charles declared.

"There is no other way, Charles, and you know it. Raina is the only one who can draw Shears out in the open and force him to play his hand."

Raina laid her hand on Charles. "You know it is the only way," she said.

Charles squeezed her hand and sighed. "I know, but it does not mean I have to enjoy it. What is the plan?"

Thorn explained to them how they would make their presence tonight at the Pennington Ball, where they could put in their first public debut as a married couple. It would send shockwaves through the ballroom, because everybody expected him to be dead, not alive and married. While they were there, they would split up and stop the attack. The Crown's agents would be in position. It was Raina's job to draw Shears out in the open. Once she did, the agents could swoop in to capture Shears, along with the other players in the game. Their plan was to be cautious, and no gentleman or lady was to be trusted.

After their plans were made, everybody made their way to prepare for the ball. Ivy was to remain at home after several persuasive arguments on her part to join them. Thorn decided Sammy would stay and keep her company until their return. More like keep her guarded. The only flaw with the plan was that Ivy had Sammy wrapped around her fingers. But with Thorn using their unborn child as the reason, she agreed to await their return.

Charles returned home to dress for the ball as Raina prepared upstairs. When Charles returned for Raina, he made his way to their room. Upon entering the bedroom, he was unprepared for the vision waiting for him. Standing in the middle of the room was his wife, dressed in the red dress he seen only a glimpse of all those months ago. The red silk hugged her body in layers. Every curve of her body was on display. The red top clung to her breasts, filling them out as they teased the imagination. Nested between her breasts was the ruby necklace he gave her. The dress dipped into her waist and hugged along her hips over her thighs, where at the bottom of her legs the dress flared out into dark red skirts.

She did not wear her hair up, but let the dark black tresses hang down her back, with one long tress curled over her shoulder. Her creamy skin glowed. Charles swallowed, tongue tied into silence. There were no words to describe how stunning she looked. She stood watching him nervously, waiting for his approval.

Raina stood anxiously waiting for him. She had dressed in a hurry. She wanted tonight over. Her nerves had never bothered her in all the months she had been in danger. But tonight was different. Raina knew she had more at stake than ever before—Charles.

When he came rushing into the bedroom and stopped in silence, she felt calm but anxious. She did not like feeling this vulnerable. He was so handsome, from his thick, wavy blond hair to the way he filled out his suit. He was everything she had always dreamed about. He took the few steps to her side. Charles reached for her gloved hand and bestowed a kiss on her knuckles.

"While I loved you in your white wedding dress, it is nothing to what I feel for you in red. You are a vision in red, my dear." He then leaned over to whisper in her ear, "I cannot wait to peel this creation from your body later. I have dreamed of you in this dress for months."

"Oh, Charles," she whispered.

He took her mouth hungrily under his and devoured her. Their kiss grew uncontrollable as their passion reached new heights. Charles wanted her now, wearing this creation of red. He wanted to feel her wetness glide him in as they comforted each other for the danger they were headed into. He knew he needed to pull back, but the fear only enticed him more. The fear of losing her drove his kisses more desperate.

Charles pulled back and tried to gain control over his emotions. He rested his forehead against hers. His hands held her cheeks in his palms. As their breaths came under control, the air between them whispered their desire and fear.

"I love you, Lady Mallory."

"I love you, Lord Mallory."

He drew her into his embrace. Her arms wrapped tightly around him as he rested his chin on top of her forehead. They stood quietly, their hearts beating in time as they savored their last moments before they had to leave.

~~~~~

When the carriage pulled up to the grand townhome, Thorn and the duke exited first and waited for Charles to help Raina from the conveyance. As they made their way to the receiving line, they waited as whispers echoed around them. Looks of shock graced the faces as they walked by.

When they were ready to be announced, the ballroom was bursting, and noise rang out from every direction. Voices could be heard as the ton gossiped and the musicians played a quadrille. When the names Lord and Lady Mallory were announced over the roar of the crowd, they were met with silence. All talking ceased and the dancers stopped in mid-step. All eyes were turned toward them as they made their way down the stairs and into the ballroom.

Lady Pennington rushed to their side, waving to the musicians to start the music again. With another wave of her hand, she directed her staff to serve the champagne. Coming before them, she curtsied to the duke.

"I am so honored you could attend my ball, Your Grace. I had heard of your son's death, but I can see for myself the falsity of the claim."

"A terrible rumor floating around the gossip ring. May I be the first to present my son's charming bride to you? Raina, our dear friend Lady Pennington."

"It is an honor to greet you. Raina is such an exotic name befitting your beauty."

"Thank you, My Lady. It is French," Raina replied.

"Well I am glad you have finally settled, you rascal," she said to Charles.

"Well, since you were taken, my dear, I conned Raina here to be my bride." He pulled Raina close to his side as he showed his affection.

"Trouble since the day he was born. Keep a close eye on this one."

"That will not be a problem," Raina murmured as she stared into Charles's eyes.

"No, I do not think it will." She turned to Thorn. "How is Ivy fairing?"

"Restless and trouble, as always," he replied.

She laughed. "Before long you will have two of them. I wish you the best. Please give her my regards, and I will visit after the child is born."

Thorn nodded. "I will let Ivy know."

They spoke more, catching up on news. After a while, she excused herself to see to her other guests. They took a small stroll around the ballroom, catching up with further acquaintances. Standing near the doors to the balcony, they paused as they sipped on their wine. They watched the crowd for any suspicious action. Thorn informed them everybody was in place.

Raina tensed next to Charles as she watched the gentleman approach. He spoke his congratulations to the couple and offered for Raina to accompany him on the next dance. She tried to make an excuse, but Charles insisted she not offend the man. So, she was left to dance the next set with Lord Craven. As they made their way to the dance floor, Raina's eyes darted around for any excuse to part company, but luck was not on her side.

"Smile, my dear. We do not want to give your husband any excuse to rescue you."

Raina smiled politely at her companion, but her body did not relax.

"Much better. Now, tonight is the night. When Maxwell arrives, you are to lead him to the gardens, where you will then execute him."

"But he is close to getting the information you need."

"His time is up; he has failed. He has proven to be a liability. One we don't want to have on our hands anymore. As per our agreement, you will kill him tonight. You will stage it as an attack and that you were defending yourself. You will have the pity of the ton at your disposal. Smart move on marrying Mallory, but do not think you are indispensable."

"But what if Maxwell does not show?"

"Oh, he will be here. I have made sure of this. Now I will return you to your besotted husband, and you will thank me prettily for the dance. Remember, if Maxwell does not die at your hands tonight, then you will die by our hands. Do I make myself clear, Lady Mallory?"

"Yes," she snarled.

Lord Craven returned her to Charles's side. Charles was busy talking to a few gentlemen and didn't watch the exchange on the dance floor. He pulled her close as he continued his conversation. After the gentlemen wandered away, he pulled her onto the dance floor for a waltz.

He held her firmly to his body as their bodies floated through the steps. Her red skirts floated between his trousers as he turned her around and around in circles, his hand along her back, lazily stroking her as they twisted and turned. When the dance was over, he still held her within his arms. Charles shocked the ton as he softly kissed her lips and whispered in her ear on what he planned to do once they were alone. Turning a dark shade of red at the display of affection, Raina could not pull away. She was too caught up in his spell.

"It is showtime, my dear," he whispered before he pulled apart from her.

Raina, lost in him, was slow to comprehend his words at first. When she finally realized what he was saying, she looked up into the crowd. She saw Shears's men filing into the ballroom. Before long, Shears would make an entrance. Then so would Maxwell. Charles pulled Raina after him as he went in search of Thorn. Raina kept her eyes trained on Shears's men. Something was not right. When she looked closer, she saw they were setting up explosives. They were attempting to blow up the ball.

Raina stopped, pulling Charles up short. When Charles turned around at her resistance, he saw where her attention was occupied. When she pointed at the explosives, Charles knew what Shears's final plan was for the night. He was going to blow up the ball and everybody who kept him from his plot. Seeing the gentlemen of the ton who were secretly involved with Shears send their loved one's home and gather at the top of the balcony, Charles panicked. He reached Thorn and his father, telling them of their findings. They needed to clear the ballroom now before anything happened.

But it was too late.

Chapter Twenty-Five

IVY HAD BEEN WAITING for hours for any news from Thorn, but none came. She had already beat Sammy at checkers multiple times. He had drifted off to sleep after eating Cook's scones. Tommy was fast asleep after the telling of multiple stories. With nobody to keep her company, Ivy wandered the house. Her nerves were on edge with this waiting. When she walked back along the hallway for what seemed the hundredth time, she came to a sudden stop, for inside the door stood Zane. The expression on his face was one of sorrow. And pity.

"No," Ivy cried before she fell.

Zane reached out to grab her before her body hit the ground. He picked her up into his arms and made his way to the library. Lying her on the couch, he held her hand until she came to. He did not mean to frighten her this way, but he wanted to be the one to inform her about Thorn. It was because of him Thorn had died.

Ivy's eyelids fluttered open. When she saw Zane, she knew it was not a dream.

"Thorn?"

"I am so sorry, Ivy, but I received news that Thorn has been killed by Shears."

"It cannot be true. I would know. I would feel if he had left me," she cried.

"It was a reliable source."

"Take me to him then."

"Ivy, it would be best if you stay here until I can find out more details."

"No, Zane Maxwell. You will take me to him this instant. If you don't, I will find my way there. So, you can either accompany me or not." Ivy struggled to rise.

Zane knew her words were true. It was probably for the best if she came with him, this way he could protect her. Ivy was in danger still. He failed her before, but this time he would not.

"Only if you agree to stay by my side the entire time."

"Agreed, we must hurry."

Zane helped Ivy to his carriage, and they made their way to the Pennington Ball. It was utter chaos. Men and women were running from the entrance, screaming about treason, explosives, and death.

Zane pulled Ivy to the side of the house, away from the mad crush of people exiting. Making their way to a side entrance, Zane led them through the back of the house to the ballroom, where the madness was took shape. Maxwell saw Shears's men and his co-conspirators gathering around the balcony. It was what he saw the men holding that made him pause. They would blow the place sky high. He had to remove Ivy from this danger. He was a fool for bringing her here.

"This way," Zane urged.

"Look, Zane, he is alive. I must get to Thorn."

Before he could stop her, she disappeared into the throng. He watched her weaving against the flow of people to get to Thorn's side. He tried to push himself to her, but he kept getting pressed back farther and farther. But before she reached Thorn, he saw Shears grab her.

He was torn. Maxwell couldn't reach Ivy, but he could put a stop to the explosion.

He backed away to take a different direction to the balcony. As he twisted around, it was to find a pistol aimed at him. It was Raina.

Her hands were shaking so badly as she pointed the gun at Maxwell. She did not want to do this. But it was the only way. It was him or her. She must do what was necessary to survive.

"You don't want to kill me, Raina."

"I have no choice. It was part of my agreement with the Crown. They said tonight, or it will be me."

"It will be you either way," he said, trying to reason with her.

"No."

"Yes, Raina. Think about it. You know as much information as I do, if not more. They are getting you to do their dirty work. They cannot kill a member of the peerage, but they can get somebody else to, and that is you. After you kill me, then they will kill you."

"No, you are lying. I am safe. I am married to Charles now."

"It will not matter to them. They will stage it as an accident. You are expendable to them."

Raina listened to Maxwell plead for his life and knew he was correct. She was nothing but a pawn to them too. First Shears, now the Crown. The only thing she knew for certain was that she wasn't a pawn with Charles. She lowered her weapon and dropped it to the floor. Maxwell reached down and slid it along the back of his trousers.

"Listen, Raina, we have little time. I need your help. I must help Thorn and Charles stop this place from being blown, and I need you to rescue Ivy from Shears."

"What is Ivy doing here?"

"You are not the only one being played for a fool. I fell for their trap tonight, and in doing so, I have put Ivy at risk. She was the goal all along this evening. You must stop them before Shears gets away with her."

With direction from Maxwell, Raina set off on her pursuit of Ivy. Making her way to the gardens, Raina heard voices in the distance—voices who were all too familiar to her. She paused behind a hedge as she listened to Shears praise Lord Craven on bringing both Ivy and Maxwell to the party. Raina thought Lord Craven worked for the Crown. She had been duped. He was another one of Shears's lackies. Who else was? How deep did this fall? Who was she to trust? Obviously, no one. Raina only trusted the small circle of her new family. Now wasn't the time to ponder though. Her only goal was to rescue Ivy. As she peeked between a small opening, it was to find Ivy's hands tied as she sat upon a bench. There was nobody else but Shears and Craven. Raina needed to cause a distraction. When she glanced around, she came up empty. The only thing to distract Shears would be herself. She would have to draw Shears away from Ivy. Stepping off to the edge of the hedge, she let out a low whistle. It was a warning whistle she heard Shears use with his men to warn of danger. Raina had learned it over the past year. She could use this to her advantage and cause his men to panic.

She watched as Shears paused. Then she whistled again, even louder than the one before. Stepping into the moonlight, she continued whistling until she came upon them.

"You," he hissed.

"Me," Raina taunted him.

"You're dead."

"No, very much alive."

"How?"

Before she answered Shears, there was a small explosion behind the house. Smoke filled the air. Shears grabbed Ivy off the bench and shoved her into Lord Craven's arms as he reached for Raina. Raina ducked, drifting away in the smoke. She heard Shears yell for Craven to help him. As they circled around looking for her, Raina made her way back to Ivy. She untied Ivy's arms and was about to make their escape when Shears blocked their path. He sneered at them as he motioned for them to follow in front of him. They had no choice but to do his bidding.

~~~~~~

Charles was beside himself. He had lost Raina in this madness. With the help from Thorn and his men, they gathered every conspirator and turned them over to the Crown—before they diffused the explosives. This only left them with capturing Shears. The man was nowhere to be seen. He was here though. Charles could feel him near. With all this destruction, Shears would want to watch his handiwork. Though he'd stopped the terror plot, he lost his wife. Pushing through the crowd, he moved in search of her. But instead of her, he ran into Maxwell.

"Where is she?" He grabbed a hold of Maxwell by his shirt.

"She is going after Ivy."

"Ivy? What is she doing here?" Thorn arrived from behind them to ask.

"It is my fault. I brought her here."

"Why the hell did you do that?"

"I can explain later. I sent Raina after her. They left toward the garden."

The three men ran toward the terrace. Taking the stairs to the garden, they spread out to look for the ladies. They did not have to go far. Shears was leading them toward the house. While Charles and Thorn stopped in front of their wives, Maxwell hid his identity from the man.

"Move no further, or I will end their lives in front of you."

They stopped where they were. Lord Craven would have no part of it.

"Now Shears, you never discussed taking hostages."

"You fool. I am only taking what I wish—this sweet package. The rest I will kill," he stated as he pulled Ivy toward him.

She whimpered her distaste for Shears, but other than that, she didn't utter a sound. She learned not to bait the captain, for that was what he desired.

"This will be high treason. I cannot abide any of this. I will not hang for you."

"What is one more act of treason than what I am already partaking in?"

"I won't be a part of this," Craven said as he moved away.

But he didn't get far before Shears raised his pistol and shot the man in the back. The double agent fell to the ground with a thud. Still, the rest did not move from their positions. They knew any sudden movement would be the cause for their own deaths.

"From what I can see, all of you have destroyed my plans for this evening. For this, I will seek my revenge on every single one of you. You will not stop me from destroying England."

"We have stopped your sources tonight, Shears. You will discover no more allies in England," Charles told him.

"That is where you are wrong, Mallory. I have contacts all throughout your country. I will rebuild my crew, and this country will suffer."

"Let the women go, Shears," Charles demanded.

"You can have this one." Shears shoved Raina into his arms. "But I will keep this one." He pulled Ivy behind him.

Thorn stood still as stone as he watched Shears manhandle Ivy. It was sheer willpower that kept him from killing the man, but he would not risk Ivy or the baby by a masculine move. He would wait for the right time to rescue her.

Charles watched from behind as Maxwell silently made his way toward Shears. He held a knife, ready to attack. He worked on distracting Shears. But before he could distract him, Raina advanced after Shears with her own knife.

When Shears saw Raina running toward him, he let go of Ivy, dropping her to the ground. As he set up his hands to block her attack, he let his prey be taken away. Thorn swept in to rescue Ivy, pulling her away from danger. Shears grabbed Raina's arms, twisting the knife from her hands. After her knife fell to the ground, he continued his assault, bending her fingers back, making her cry out in pain. Then lifted his arms back to smack her when he was shoved from the side.

As Charles waved for Thorn to take Ivy away, he advanced on Shears. As Shears brought his arm back to smack Raina, his head rammed him in the side. Shears staggered as he caught hold of Raina's skirts, dragging her to the ground with him. As he watched Raina struggle to escape his clutches, she kicked her foot across his face. But still Shears didn't release Raina. He twisted her leg, causing her to scream.

Her hands fought against his clutches. Her fingers scratching at his arms, but still he didn't let up on bending her leg back. She kicked him with her other foot. Between her struggles with Shears, Charles finally pulled him off her with Maxwell's help. Once free from him, she tried to rise, but the pain in her leg kept her from moving.

As Maxwell held onto Shears, Charles was uncontrollable, landing blow after blow on Shears. The man only laughed after each time Charles punched him. This only enticed Mallory more. He wanted this man dead for what his family has endured at his hands. He wanted him to suffer as much as Raina had suffered, but it wasn't enough.

"Charles, stop. Stop." He faintly heard Raina's cries as he continued his blows.

"Get her out of here. I've got him," Maxwell ordered.

"Charles," Raina tried to get his attention again.

He stopped, looking over at her. She lay on the ground, her dress torn to shreds. Tears streaking down her face. Her hand clutching at her leg. She was injured. He dropped his hold on Shears and went to her side. Lifting her in his arms, he turned back to Maxwell.

"Go now," Maxwell shouted.

Charles left the garden with Raina in his arms. When he turned back around to Maxwell, it was to witness his friend pummeling his enemy. When Shears tried to fight back, Maxwell stuck his knife into the man's side. Maxwell stood back as the man dropped to the ground. Charles felt relief when Shears finally met his end.

But the relief was finished before it even began. Before Charles realized what was happening, Shears's men set upon Maxwell. They beat him senseless. They lifted Shears and carried him away. After they were done with Maxwell, they carried him away too.

Charles stepped forward to help his friend. Raina's touch stopped him.

"They will kill us."

"I must help him."

"We will rescue him, but now isn't the time. We are outnumbered."

Charles knew she spoke the truth. He must get her medical help and see to Ivy. He would figure out a rescue plan for his friend. Maxwell had shown his true colors tonight. While misguided, he came through for his friends. Now it was only right they come through for him.

Chapter Twenty-Six

CHARLES SAT BY RAINA'S bed as she slept. He watched her as she dozed. The morning sun was peeking through the curtains. She'd slept in peace through most of the evening. The doctor gave her laudanum for her sprained leg. When he saw Shears's handprints on her leg, it set him off in a rage. But with her gentle words, he calmed down. She was safe from danger, and that was what mattered.

The rest of England was safe from Shears too. Over the course of the evening, Shears's cronies had been gathered up and locked away in the tower. Their families were to be stripped of their titles and lands. His resources were dried up. While he had made his escape, there were agents dispatched over the entire country who were looking for information on where he traveled next. There would be no safe refuge for him. Thorn's man Jake shipped out to look for him this morning. But Charles had an idea where he might go next.

For now though, he was only concerned about his wife. They could finally put this nightmare behind them and move on with their lives. A life he planned to spoil her with. There wouldn't be a day that went by she wasn't loved by him.

Raina drifted awake, feeling groggy. Her eyelids were heavy, and her body did not want to move. She looked at Charles sitting in a chair watching her.

"Are you drugging me now?" Her attempt at humor failed. He frowned.

"Not by choice, my dear."

She tried to sit but needed his help.

"Did you find him?"

"No."

She sighed at this news. The man was forever a ghost, here one minute, gone the next. Was there any stopping him?

"We will find him."

"Maxwell?"

"We think Shears is keeping him captured."

"We will get him."

"No, we will not. We will stay in bed until we are healed."

"Charles ..."

"No, it is final. I won't put your life at risk anymore. You are too valuable to me."

"But ..."

"No, Raina."

Raina did not argue. She realized it was pointless right now. She would wait until she felt better and could persuade him. She lifted the covers for him.

"Will you at least join me?"

Charles knew she was only humoring him. Smiling, he slid under the blankets with her, pulling her into his embrace. She sighed as his arms tightened around her. He was careful not to nudge her leg as he softly caressed her. Rolling her over, he leaned above her and gently kissed her lips.

"I thought I lost you last night."

Raina reached up and brushed her hand across his cheek. She saw the fear in his eyes. She didn't know how to reassure him. Life was unpredictable. She had learned that. It never went the way you wanted it, and then one day everything fell into place. Everything clicked. It was always changing, and she learned you had to learn to change with it. Then everything would be fine. She could not take away his fears, but she could embrace them. It was part of love. With love came unwanted emotions sometimes. But she would never trade their love for anything.

"I am here." Her eyes spoke her unspoken thoughts to him. He recognized in her eyes the same fear as his, but their love would keep them safe.

"Yes, you are."

They lay there through the morning, lost in their own love. With soft kisses and touches, they spent the day adrift in their feelings for one another. When she needed to rest, he held her in his arms, offering her the comfort she needed. When she awoke, they made love again as their passions flared, each of them giving the love the other needed. Love. Trust. Understanding.

Epilogue

LATE THE NEXT MORNING they made their way to Thorn and Ivy's suite of rooms. Ivy was bedridden for the rest of her pregnancy. They visited with her, making sure she was well. They told her of their plans to find their own place. While the ladies chatted about baby names, the men sat around the fire watching the women they loved. Over the course of the last year, they had suffered a lot. But in the end, love had won.

"I realize it is the elephant in the room, but how are you going to locate Maxwell?" Ivy asked.

"Ivy, that man should be the least of your concerns. If not for him, you wouldn't be at risk today."

Thorn's comment silenced Ivy for all of two seconds. "Well?" she pushed.

Thorn growled his dislike at the concern Ivy felt for Maxwell. Damn that man. He still held his charm over her, obviously.

"One of Shears's cohorts in the tower has talked," explained Charles.

"Did you discover where he is going?" Raina asked.

"It appears he is delivering a shipment in Edinburgh."

"Do you believe this is where he is taking Maxwell?" asked Ivy.

"Yes," replied Charles.

"So, we will wait for him there," Raina stated.

Thorn laughed. "I am glad to see you married a hard head like me, my friend."

This time it was Charles who growled. "No, we won't."

Before Raina objected, Thorn took pity on his friend. "I have just the person who can infiltrate Shears's ship and rescue Maxwell. I have already sent word. As soon as contact is made, we will rescue him. In the meantime, we will wait."

"What about Shears?" Raina asked

"The person will finish Shears too. Within a few weeks, Shears will meet his maker," Thorn explained.

With that thought, they felt a sense of relief that life was secure for the next few weeks. Thorn and Ivy imagined the new addition to their family. Charles and Raina dreamed of their new life they were starting. Raina looked on at the glow of Ivy as she talked excitedly of her baby. She couldn't wait for that to be her. To give Charles a child. When she glanced up, she caught him looking at her and smiling his charming smile, which only meant one thing. She shook her head at him in rebuke, and his smile only grew larger. Charles had seen the expression Raina was getting in her eyes as she watched Ivy. He read her thoughts. She was thinking of having a child. As he caught her eyes, he sent her the signal he was willing to try. When she blushed again, he knew she was thinking the same thing. Rising from the chair, he held his hand out to her. They made their goodbyes and swiftly left to return to their bedroom. They were newlyweds, after all.

~~~~~

Look for Zane Maxwell's story in *Rescued By the Scot*

"Thank you for reading Rescued By the Spy. Gaining exposure as an independent author relies mostly on word-of-mouth, so if you have the time and inclination, please consider leaving a short review wherever you can."

*Visit my website **www.lauraabarnes.com** to join my mailing list.*

Author Laura A. Barnes

International selling author Laura A. Barnes fell in love with writing in the second grade. After her first creative writing assignment, she knew what she wanted to become. Many years went by with Laura filling her head full of story ideas and some funny fish songs she wrote while fishing with her family. Thirty-seven years later, she made her dreams a reality. With her debut novel *Rescued By the Captain*, she has set out on the path she always dreamed about.

When not writing, Laura can be found devouring her favorite romance books. Laura is married to her own Prince Charming (who for some reason or another thinks the heroes in her books are about him) and they have three wonderful children and two sweet grandbabies. Besides her love of reading and writing, Laura loves to travel. With her passport stamped in England, Scotland, and Ireland; she hopes to add more countries to her list soon.

While Laura isn't very good on the social media front, she loves to hear from her readers. You can find her on the following platforms:

You can visit her at *www.lauraabarnes.com* to join her mailing list.

Website: **http://www.lauraabarnes.com**
Amazon: **https://amazon.com/author/lauraabarnes**
Goodreads: **https://www.goodreads.com/author/show/16332844.Laura_A_Barnes**
Facebook: **https://www.facebook.com/AuthorLauraA.Barnes/**
Instagram: **https://www.instagram.com/labarnesauthor/**
Twitter: **https://twitter.com/labarnesauthor**
BookBub: **https://www.bookbub.com/profile/laura-a-barnes**

Desire other books to read by Laura A. Barnes

Enjoy these other historical romances:

Matchmaking Madness Series:

How the Lady Charmed the Marquess

Tricking the Scoundrels Series:

Whom Shall I Kiss... An Earl, A Marquess, or A Duke?

Whom Shall I Marry... An Earl or A Duke?

I Shall Love the Earl

The Scoundrel's Wager

The Forgiven Scoundrel

Romancing the Spies Series:

Rescued By the Captain

Rescued By the Spy

Rescued By the Scot